Vist

&

Proper Ganda

Book 3 in the Vist series

ANKA B. TROITSKY

July 2023

Copyright © 2023 Anka B. Troitsky
Published in UK by Greystone Consultancy LTD
NSBN: 978-1-7391959-4-6

DEDICATION

to all the victims of the war

iii

CONTENTS

*"My grandfather knew exactly what he must die for.
And I only know that I must die."*

From a letter of a Russian soldier. Earth. 2022.

1. Elya

"What would you feel if you lost your home and homeland forever? Hard to imagine. Isn't it?

"Time to open your eyes and look around. Yes. You see a blazing hell everywhere. This hell was once a solar system. And now the red giant, swollen so much that it swallowed up its planets, no longer looks like the gentle sun that woke the birds in the morning and warmed the apples in the orchards. Earth is no more, but not all of its children died with it. Let's fast-forward there ... towards the constellation that earthlings called Lyra. They wouldn't recognise it, though. So much has passed that even the positions of the stars would look different. But here, nearly a million light years away, an ageing red dwarf is drifting in the universe. It is smaller than the sun and may have been known to earthlings as Kepler's Object of Interest. It is now called Vitricus ('stepfather' in Latin) or just 'Vitr.' Several planets revolve around it, and one, slightly larger than the Earth, turned out to have an orbit in the Goldilocks zone. What does that mean? That's right. The water on it is liquid, and life is quite possible. It determined the choice of our ancestors. Now, we live on this planet, but how harsh and cruel it turned out to be! No wonder its name is Noverca, which means stepmother.

"Noverca is too close to Vitr, an M-class star, and it rotates around it synchronously. Astronomers call this kind of rotation a tidal lock. After the lesson, look at your terminals if you have forgotten the scientific definition – it's at the eighth site of the O'Teka Astronomical Encyclopedia, file fourteen. Once upon a time a satellite called the Moon revolved around the Earth in the same way – earthlings could always see only one side. So Noverca, in one journey around Vitricus, barely has time to spin on its axis, and some Earth words here have acquired a different meaning. "North" and "south" have nothing to do with the poles. The colonists called the place in direct sunlight the south, and the opposite side is called the north. One side is always facing Vitr, and it is too hot on this "dayside" of Noverca. Only ocean currents cool it a little. And in the north – on the night side – permafrost and darkness reign.

"The mainland of Gera – our new home – is closer to the eternal twilight regions. For earthlings, it has become a fixed mid-morning ... or early evening – whichever they prefer. It turned out that it is possible but difficult to live here: there is heat, strong winds, radiation and not so much oxygen in the atmosphere.

"When the first ships with settlers arrived, an earthling would not have survived even an hour outside. But people didn't come empty-handed. If you don't take care of yourself, no one else will. This time, you will learn about artificial evolution. Let's start with a brief history of genetic engineering."

The mechanic yawned, watching this lesson for the hundredth time, and so he turned away from the spherical screen in the holographic classroom below his cabin. In the audience chairs, he could see the uniform caps of two dozen nine-year-olds in jackets from the Altyn School, named after Captain Thomas Darkwood. The recording of the lecturer's voice would turn itself off after twenty minutes. The mechanic stretched and stood up from his desk. He left the cabin and went to the window, where he could see the city's entire western quarter.

He saw smoke instantly. In a straight black column, it rose to the top of the spherical dome and spread under it along the ceiling, forming an umbrella shape. The mechanic estimated the distance and decided that the fire was far enough from the temple, so he didn't raise the alarm. Instead, he raised his hand to where the epaulette-like device rested on his shoulder and activated his personal amulet to listen to the news. Between the mechanic's face and the view from the window, a translucent three-dimensional screen the size of a newspaper sheet appeared.

The speaker inside his ear beeped softly, and the young man heard an even male voice finishing the sentence, "... just seven minutes ago. Please remain calm. We have not yet been informed of possible casualties. So far, only one building is on fire, but the ordermen have controlled the reaction and isolated the room with power shields. We just received confirmation that this is oxidation and not plasma. The officers have blocked air access to the burning surfaces. So now ... any second."

And indeed, the lower part of the smoke bundle was cut off, as if by a blade, and the fuzzy end soared to the smoky cloud under the dome. There, the black mass swayed and calmed down.

Meanwhile, the soft voice of the newsman was replaced by the hoarse bass of the famous loader named General King. "Attention, citizens! To remove smoke from under the protective field, we will have to turn off the generator for a maximum of 3.6 minutes. Please close your windows if you are indoors. If you are outside, then take action. Outside the city an unfavourable level of radiation is raining down. We will start promptly at 2.15 p.m."

The mechanic checked the time. 2.08 p.m. There can't be one person in the city now who hasn't connected to the breaking news. This announcement would have come automatically if the young man had not activated his amulet. He ran around on his floor and checked the windows. He heard that the head of the sports section was doing the same on the level below and the priestess of art on the level above him. He heard the last warning, went to the window again, and saw how the dome's blue projection of an earthly sky was disappearing, as if someone had set fire to it too. An inky, overcast sky appeared over the city; a downpour hissed, and on the south side, under the clouds and in orange stripes, the crimson eye of Vitricus hung, with its rays painting the clouds' bellies a dirty yellow.

The wind blew away the smoke from the fire. The infernal vision disappeared in less than five minutes, and the city became light and sunny as before. The newly appeared dome again projected a blue sky with white clouds. Only someone had also added a rainbow to it.

Robotic neutralisers scuttled across the wet city, and the mechanic returned to the classroom and sat down at his desk in the operator cabin.

"Thank you all for your attention, and you will receive your homework tomorrow. You have to choose the topics you need to improve on. You must upload the list to the temple no later than 8.00 p.m. See you tomorrow and have a nice cycle," the half-metallic voice said. All lectures in the temple were recorded in the voice of the architexter himself. Or herself. They say it increased pupils' attention.

Below, the translucent lecture room also lit up, and a motley flock of children hurried through the doorway into the next classroom. The terrenians with purple skin, as if sprinkled with microscale sequins, and real uzhans – tall, graceful and covered with scaly heat and radiation-reflecting plates. Elya the mechanic was only half-uzhan and inherited his height from his nordian father. He spotted a couple of ikhtees, who can now reside in the water. They wore tight-fitting suits with transparent half-masks like oxygen masks but full of water. The juvenile ikhtees could spend only half a cycle on the surface before returning to the ocean. The mechanic barely made out the two hypertrichosed nordians because of their small stature. Their faces were still clean-shaven, and they would soon have to decide which beard style to pick.

All were descendants of earthlings, divided into new races depending on their chosen method of artificial adaptation. Perhaps just a small handful of the original earthlings from the second evacuation wave on Noverca, who had extended their lives, remained. The loaders. Plus their very few direct descendants. Their most effective adaptation to the planet's conditions was non-hereditary. It depended on technology and surgical support. Fortunately, they could accelerate regeneration and tolerate intervention relatively easily.

Elya sighed. He knew a lot about the loaders' descendants. He was in love with one of them, a girl named Phoebe.

Every pupil has rectangular school terminals, since amulets are issued to colonists only at the age of fifteen when they choose a personal purpose – the meaning of life, a calling, a significance ... call it what you will. Basically their chosen destiny.

The mechanic sighed again. Just a few years ago, he went from class to class this same way and kept wondering, thinking and waiting for that long-awaited interest to flare up inside. He had been interested in working with technology, but he also loved to collect musical compositions with Mozart –

the computer program that had replaced Bach over the past decade. But when he purchased a round epaulette-like amulet, he felt that improving the next generation of amulets would become his purpose. That same cycle, he applied to Master Johanna for the position of apprentice. One cycle he would become a master himself, but he was still far from opening his own factory. That's why he had to work at school. He maintained school equipment for presentations and interactive practical work for four hours per cycle, and he drew new amulet schemes in his head for the rest of his time.

The first colonists' amulets were simple medals usually hung around the neck. Only scouts wore these devices in their ears or wrists. But after a first loader remade their amulet and fitted it to a partially shaved head, a fashion for all kinds of forms began. The modern amulet became the size of a button and was worn in beads, rings, brooches and buckles. But Elya would come up with one that can be inserted inside the eyeball. Even the loaders would envy him.

The young inventor glanced at the picture of O'Teka's temple on the wall. Since geostationary satellites had been put into orbit, even distance was not a problem for common signals. If, in the past, people's amulets could access the temple only within the White Capital, now other cities were connected to the main storage. And only between major settlements are there still blind zones, but he will solve this problem too. He will—

The door to the cabin banged open.

"Elya, hey! Elya, are you there? Did you see the fire?"

One of the priestesses entered the cabin. Elya turned on the light and saw an anxious young face.

"I'm here, Pettle. I saw it. What was on fire? Not a residential building, I hope?"

"No, it was a factory. Elya ..."

There was only one factory in that direction: the Da Costa ecoblocks for breeding sand beetles. It would be a pity if the bugs rose in price or disappeared from stores altogether.

And then it hit him like a thunderbolt. Phoebe had been working there for the last few months as an apprentice.

He jumped up.

"Are there any casualties?"

"They didn't say yet. Don't you know someone there?"

Mechanic Elya Goryn was already running to the elevator. He fell, and when he got up, he didn't pay attention to the sharp pain in his foot. He ran fast, but the panic in him grew even faster.

2. Toffee Shop

All passers-by fled from Market Street towards the fire. The artificial but moderate sunlight grew even dimmer in the smoky air. A brown poodle with silver eyes sneezed discontentedly on the porch of a shoe store.

Not far from the burning building, a woman wearing a yellow headscarf was walking calmly along an almost deserted street behind a small toffee shop. Of the other passers-by, only another woman, an older woman, was walking a few steps behind, rocking a swaddled bundle in her arms.

As she reached the back of the store, the woman in the yellow headscarf suddenly turned pale. She screamed and fell but was caught by a strong hand under her elbow.

"It's all right, my girl ... You're fine. Come with me. You'll feel better now. The nausea will pass quickly. Trust me, I'm a mother."

The older woman released her elbow and pushed the door while still holding the bundle, but rather casually, almost under her arm. She entered the house and dragged the still-swaying woman inside. She laid the bundle on one armchair, seated the younger woman on another, and looked into her eyes.

"Feeling sick?" she asked sympathetically.

"Yes. May I have some water?"

"Of course, your condition is understandable. Also, the smoke and the stench of burning have carried here. It's even making me dizzy."

After the woman in the yellow headscarf drank water and her cheeks regained their usual purple blush, she finally stopped swaying.

"I didn't think it would be so scary."

"It's only scary the first time. Next time will be easier."

"I don't want to any more. No more times for me."

"Well, only God knows that. If you have to do it again ..."

"No, someone else better do it," said the younger one, and they both laughed a little. "It feels so weird. Your body no longer belongs to you. You are a vessel for someone else, and you are no longer in control."

"Well, yes, but what can I say? We must do what we must. Don't worry. You'll feel better. I'll see to it. They need at least an hour to remove the radiation after closing the dome. You'll have to wait here before going home. Rest, and I'll cook both of us something nice to eat."

Soon the room was filled with the delicious smell of melted cheese, and the woman got up, covered the motionless bundle in the chair with her yellow shawl, and went to the window. Outside, it would be dark for a few minutes, and the rain pounded on the canvas trading tents.

3. Factory

Even in a society as unusual as the colony on Gera, people are curious and highly receptive to unexpected events. Fires rarely happen here since negligence and imprudence are not common, even among young residents. There are mistakes and shortcomings, but arson? No one has remembered this happening for a long time. And that's why almost all the curious gathered at the blackened building were sure that an accident had occurred. Nothing else came to mind.

The factory building itself didn't have enough time to burn down. The soot repainted it from silver to black, the doors were ruined and there were no windows. That was why this misfortune was not noticed immediately, and the alarm was raised after the fire had burned out the interior.

A few ordermen came out of the building and immediately activated their amulets. Their group of five resembled a giant flower with the glassy petals of their oval holoscreens. The enforcers reported the badly damaged offices and warehouses to O'Teka. They were so preoccupied that they almost missed a twenty-five-year-old man who came out of the crowd of onlookers and rushed through the dark doorway. One of the officers grabbed him by his grey work gown. "Hey, stop! It's not safe there …"

But the gown was immediately thrown off and left in the officer's hands.

Elya knew the location of the premises in the factory better than the ordermen. When two of them rushed after him, into the remnants of smoke and darkness, they didn't see him running straight to the "dunes."

Master Rod Baker was the first to name the insectariums "dunes." Each dune was a well-insulated hall of about 0.6 hectares, domed with a holo-screen that simulated the Earth days and seasons of Welsh beaches around the clock. It was there on Earth that the first sand beetles were originally bred at the end of the twenty-eighth century.

The colony's technology made it possible to maintain the necessary temperature in the halls, the daily light fluctuations, the seasonal changes in a year on Earth with the corresponding precipitation and even the desired water salinity. It would be convenient for the sandies to grow and fatten without all these tricks, but they were very fussy about their reproduction conditions. They demanded the golden sun at its zenith, fresh sea air and lower temperatures no matter what.

When Elya entered the first dune, he faced a terrible sight. The dome's laser screen no longer showed night or noon. A gaping hole in a burst membrane of the ceiling allowed in the city light and made it possible to see grey sand studded with motionless black dots. Elya took a couple of steps on the sand, and something crunched under his foot. He bent down and picked up a round corpse the size of a walnut. It seems that when the temperature of the water and sand increased, the beetles climbed to the surface, where they were also showered with radioactive rain. They couldn't take much.

Elya dropped the dead beetle and hurried to the next hall.

He soon found out that the membrane had remained intact in two insectariums out of six, but the water hadn't heated up as much in just one. Here, if the beetles didn't survive, several kilograms of larvae could still be saved. It seems that the duty watcher – the fire's main victim – also thought that. The flame apparently overtook her while trying to barricade the corridor with a power shield. She caught fire and ran like a flaming torch into the middle of the dune, trying to get to the artificial surf, but fell just a few steps into the water.

Elya sat down in horror near the charred body. He already knew this was not his beloved, the tall and narrow-shouldered Phoebe Baker. So it wasn't her shift. However, Elya couldn't immediately decide which of the Da Costas had died in this fire.

In front of him lay a short nordian on her side, surrounded by the sickening smell of completely burned hair and easily wounded flesh. Da Costa, Scarlett and Harlow were always hard to tell apart. But now it was too scary to look closely and a bit too dark in the smoke. Elya felt sick.

An orderman approached him, took him by the elbow, and put him on his feet, Elya dutifully went out with him into the fresh air and, with relief, inhaled deeply. He coughed again when he saw who that orderman was exactly. General Mikael King himself stood in front of him in his uniform and a mask. He no longer paid attention to Elya, but instead ordered his subordinates. They carried out orders promptly and coherently. Someone was carrying a stretcher with a body bag to the building, and someone was unloading thermal containers to rescue sandies. Elya heard a creaky voice with a strong earthy accent. Apparently, Master Baker was also giving orders here from the speaker of someone's amulet. A very expensive conmot – a colony vehicle powered by the ZP energy converter – drove up to the site in front of the factory, and two figures got out. Elya thankfully recognised Phoebe, who immediately, without even noticing him, headed for the dunes and attached her amulet to a protective helmet.

"I know that it's not higher than fourteen, daddy. Jaxon is on his way here too. Calm down. We'll do what can be done." She had a business tone with a bitter note. Elya knew that Phoebe would grieve and cry later.

The second figure that came out of the conmot didn't run anywhere, didn't fuss, and didn't give orders. They were dressed in a wide dark robe made of the strongest ucha-silk, like the gear that the field scouts wore. This person's hands were pushed into long sleeves. The hood was thrown back. Dark-red curls fell to the right shoulder, but the left temple was bare. Above the ear was a dark crescent-shaped amulet plate on which a tiny blue spark blinked.

The crowd of onlookers, who didn't disperse in any way, fell silent. Elya knew well that before him stood his top employer, the architexter, the chief priest of the Temple of O'Teka, a real earthling, one of the second-wave settlers, the first loader of Noverca, and the last loader of the Earth, with a short name – Vist.

Elya knew a lot about loaders but always felt he didn't understand the most important thing about them. Although a whole population of loaders now lived in the colony, no one would call them a race. They didn't have much in common. All that united them was that they were created artificially and used to be people. In addition to living organic tissues, they were stuffed with a mass of metal and nano polymers, which were not just replacement prostheses, but entire computer consoles. And yet, these were not machines or cyborgs but living individuals capable of not only ordinary feelings but also feelings unknown to others. Their living cells regularly regenerated, but not at all like those of mere mortals. And this was not a figure of speech. Loaders aged differently and could decide how long to live and with what benefits loaded into them. Some carried complex amounts of knowledge in their heads; others were especially strong at dexterity and endurance. Others, like walking laboratories, could perform molecular analyses of samples in the wild regions of Noverca right on the spot.

Elya also knew that no one was born a loader. They had to be created artificially out of a living person. And not necessarily from the living. And not necessarily from one.

Some time ago, Phoebe had told Elya to keep a secret – that the second loader of Noverca lives in Pettogreko and was a master culinary specialist named Obydva. He was made up of two people. One was one of Phoebe's fathers, but Obydva's mind was not his. It was the result of an "upload." Phoebe couldn't explain what that was. It happened when she was only four years old.

As for the architexter themself, they were completely shrouded in mystery and obscurity. Elya knew more legends than facts. It was said that Vist was a man who had undertaken a special vow or was on a great mission and lived in seclusion, serving the pristine goddess O'Teka. And yet another equally valid opinion was that Vist was a woman, not just a loader but the physical embodiment of O'Teka herself. She was artificially created, of course, because she knew everything that the temple keeps, everything that the whole humanity of the Earth knew. Or at least what was written in the earthly "bibles," that is novercians word for books. Most of the colonists were big sceptics, and Elya was sure that it was all related to the architexter's ability to obtain almost instant access to any information.

An ordinary colonist could also delve into the archives of his deity – humanity's knowledge and experience – but only in the first nine levels and those for which he was deemed qualified enough. That would take time. For example, to learn one of the ancient languages or the history of some earthly era, you would have to spend many cycles in a temple or work with an amulet. In contrast, Vist could blink and come up with a result in less than a second ... or, in the worst case scenario, in a few minutes. It would take at least a quarter of an hour for the other priests of the temple to just find the correct bible in O'Teka. They were far from Vist. That is, unless Timofey Hesley, an apprentice of the architexter, could achieve his master's level and become a high loader.

Elya thought Vist would also enter the factory building, but he or she just stood in front of the main entrance and silently looked at the blackened walls. The side where the service premises and offices were located suffered the most, and not only from the fire. When trying to extinguish it, projectors of power shields were hastily installed here. Apparently, the field hit the wall, so the front and the main entrance looked especially pitiful. A huge piece of the shell flew off one of the walls that had been doodled and painted on by local children of several generations, and the melted insulation, soot, and dents from the shields left almost nothing of the scribbled quatrains and drawings of large and small beetles, primitive landscapes, houses and hearts.

Vist looked at the graffiti for a long time, then turned and walked back to the conmot.

General King was already there, and he asked the architexter, "Will you go to the temple or go home?"

"What is Steven saying?" replied the loader in an even, androgenous voice with a metallic undertone.

"Steven confirmed that Scarlett was fine. She was already on her way home, but now Steve will take her to Dr Darkwood."

"He's doing the right thing. So we're going to New Tokyo too."

Elya watched the crowd of onlookers making way for the architexter's conmot for a minute, then went to find Phoebe in the dunes to offer her all possible   help.

4. Borders

The white-walled capital's dome cannot be seen from Salty Village on the shore of the north-western Laguna. It would take at least eight hours of hiking before a transparent bubble would be visible above the treeline, and only if the clouds dropped low.

Two almost identically dressed villagers approached the colony's border, where a farmer was waiting for them. The villagers' faces and hands were smeared with white clay to protect them from Vitr's radiation. The farmer struggled to see the difference between them until they came closer. She seemed at least fifty years old. Her short but muscular figure was dressed in wildland travel clothes that protected her from excess radiation and heat. And on her head was a leather travelling helmet the same colour as her lavender face.

They greeted her and stared hungrily at the four big green bags she was unloading from her truck. A row of border posts stretched to the right and left, and only a furrow in the black grass indicated the active force field separating the villagers from the colony's territory.

"Have you brought what I ordered?" the farmer asked.

One of the villagers, the older man with a bald, scaly head, who was dressed in a knee-length pale knitted tunic, threw a whitish bag off his shoulder and untied it.

"Of course. But ... Five trees died a couple of months ago in the grove under the hills, so we have a crop failure. I brought only eleven pears."

"We agreed on twenty. Show me."

The man took out the bag and showed the woman an oblong vessel almost a litre in volume – brown, wrinkled and a large dried fruit. The top of the pear had been cut off and smeared with the hardened wax of pink fungi.

"Didn't dilute it this time, I swear," the villager added.

"That's good. But, Gafan! For eleven pears, I can't give you everything you asked for." The farmer shrugged. "You came with a friend, so you expected to carry everything away."

The villager named Gafan looked back at the gloomy younger man who had been standing silently behind him.

"What are you holding on to this time?" Gafan asked, staring again at the bags by the farmer's feet.

"Take cheese and canned vegetables, coffee too, and even antibiotics with antiseptics, but I won't give you a radiavitiser with a personal diagno-device. It's equipment, I can still get in trouble for it."

The silent one poked Gafan in the side, and he reluctantly shook his head at the farmer.

"No, that won't do. Karlina, I'll try to collect more and make up the shortfall next time. Or let's leave the food."

After bargaining for a couple of minutes, the parties agreed, and the farmer approached one of the pillars. She took out a torch-like object from her belt, pointed it at the villagers with one hand, and put the other on a pole, or rather, on an oval biometric reader the size of her palm.

"Only you," she said, "and your friend doesn't move. Understood? First, you alone will drag everything over the line."

Gafan nodded, and when the field between the two pillars disappeared, he stepped over its print in the grass, put the sack of pears on the ground, and picked up two rather heavy green bags.

At that moment, the silent villager took off, rushed towards the farmer, and was thrown back as if by a powerful push of air. Stunned, he fell on his back, and Gafan froze with the bags and his feet on opposite sides of the border.

The farmer's face showed annoyance. "That's it then. I knew it. Move before you're cut in two."

Gafan quickly moved his foot to his side and lowered the bags to the ground.

The farmer loaded her goods and pears into the truck as soon as the field was restored.

Gafan checked his friend was alive and called out to the woman, "I didn't know, I swear. I asked him to help me."

"You are a fool, Gafan. Did you really think I wouldn't guess that you didn't order things for yourself that you don't even know how to use? Who were you in the colony before we met? You never studied medicine before buying your shop."

The farmer closed the luggage compartment and turned to the villager.

Gafan was confused. He mumbled, "Martyr will punish me."

"I don't care what Contagione does to you. I need a reliable supplier of dream pears, but you are unreliable. Right. I am going now. Your friend will wake up in about twenty minutes, and for now, at least keep the flies away from him. They will devour him."

Gafan waved his purple hands.

"Karlina, wait ... wait, I will be right back."

He ran a few steps behind the dark-blue bushes at the turn in the road and returned with a second bag, which he had hidden on the way to the rendezvous point.

"Here," he said joyfully as he caught his breath and nodded at the unconscious person. "He persuaded me to hide half."

"Stay there."

The farmer herself unloaded, carried the remaining packages abroad, and caught the bag Gafan threw to her. But before reactivating the field, she opened one of the pears, drank from it and left the pear with the remains in the grass for Gafan.

"If you stay alive, come along on the eve of the new calendar with your pears. I'll bring you a copy if it comes out in souvenir format. And if you allow yourself one more trick, our business relationship will end there too. Understood?"

Gafan nodded and said, "Say hello for me to—"

"Yes, yes ... I know!"

When the farmer left, Gafan picked up a pear-shaped flask left for him and took a sip. He broke off a branch from a dark tree, sat beside his young comrade, and brushed the goon-fly from the dusty face. He would very much like to get out of here as soon as possible, but he knew he could not manage the delivery of all the contraband to the village. Nor could he return without the product.

Getting a few cuffs here was better than disappointing the Great Martyr.

5. Cemetery

The desert to the south of the colony had become a graveyard a very long time ago. In the very centre of the crimson rocky expanse, almost a hundred metres tall, stood a long and narrow object that looked like a giant demon sword. It could be seen from any edge of the desert and served as the main landmark. It was a fragment of an antenna from Noverca's first unsuccessfully launched artificial satellite. Other pieces fell into the ocean, but this one pierced the very heart of the desert and remained standing, almost at a right angle.

This attempt was made some time after the second wave of colonists arrived and shortly before the first loader, and his team, returned.

And when the first project initiator, Professor Rig Perch, died, he was buried according to his will in the centre of this crimson square, right beneath the upright remains of his creation, as though under a tree. A couple of generations later, his widow, brother and both sons lay by his side.

Previously, all the deceased colonists were taken to the scientific facilities. It was almost ceremonial since these were times of great demand for any genetic and donor materials important for the colonists and the survival of the human tribe. Then the useless remains would be turned into a handful of dust by an energy converter and placed in an urn. At first, the urns were stored in the temple. On Professor Perch's initiative, they were moved to the crimson square and placed in a spiral around a tall monument. The life expectancy of the colonists on Noverca was almost three times longer than that of Earth inhabitants. Nevertheless, only the loaders had not died on the planet yet.

For many decades, according to a strange, almost Earth-like tradition, the remains of respected colonists were brought here with honours, and the spiral of small sepulchres gradually grew. But the main memories and their "eternal lives" were stored in the reliable hands of O'Teka. Anyone could honour the departed by referring to their works, knowledge, discoveries, achievements and inventions uploaded to the temple's database. The number of colonists who lived without purpose and didn't offer O'Teka anything worthwhile was negligible. Each person who achieved something recorded it in the archives of the temple, contributed to the general knowledge of humanity, and forever gained eternal life in the history of civilisation.

On the cycle of Harlow Da Costa's farewell ritual, the spiral path around the monument became one step longer, and a new hole for the urn was burned into the red stone by a zapper. An hour later, a polymer seal with a built-in holoprojector bearing the name, dates and O'Teka's file number was visible on the surface.

Harlow's mourners had already departed, Vist took away old Baker and the weeping Scarlett in their conmot, and only Phoebe, Elya and Groonya remained at the grave. The girls sat on a stone still unclaimed by the cemetery, their legs outstretched and their backs leaning against each other. Their dark silhouettes cast long shadows on the red desert. Elya, with his conbike, stood in the shadow near Phoebe's open conmot and wondered what geological phenomenon could have created such a strange formation. It could be worth looking for a prayer about this in the temple. This stone area may be flat because it used to be a lake of liquid lava. The wind and endless sand rushing over it only polished the red stone, and the cracks were formed by new noverquakes and the movement of the crust.

Elya's thoughts were interrupted by another cry from Groonya, "What did poor Harlow have to offer in such a short life? A few recipes for Jaxon's collection?"

"But what recipes!" Phoebe replied. "Even Dad was delighted and positively impressed. And don't forget the new water pump design, four love stories ... and her poetry?"

Groonya was silent for a minute and gasped, "O'Teka! I am so blank! Cadro Lipietto! I almost forgot that I wanted to visit his grave after the ceremony. He was my favourite poet!"

She stood up and touched the amulet on the wide bracelet on her left wrist. About forty metres away, a full-length holographic image of the uzhan, in a tailcoat and with his hand raised to Vitr, soared above one of the sepulchres. Groonya walked towards him between the graves, stepping over sections of the spiral path, and then Phoebe turned to Elya.

Elya once again thought how different the sisters were, after all. Groonya is only a few years older, but she was the cloned daughter of one of the two fathers – Rod Baker – while Phoebe was born from an artificially assembled zygote with the genetic material of both men. She had light-brown hair, not black. She, in her youth, too, was graceful, like Master Baker, but her height was truly outstanding. Especially next to the nordians. The top of Elya's head barely reached her shoulder, but that wasn't the problem. Phoebe could look down on Elya even while sitting on the ground.

"I told you she's shy around strangers ... don't wait for us," Phoebe said.

"Am I a stranger?" Elya was offended.

"For her, everybody is a stranger if they do not reside in Altyn District."

"I just wanted to show my support."

"We'll be fine. Go home. We won't be going to Altyn tonight anyway."

Phoebe and her sister were very different from their peers. They were almost unmodified earthlings, with nearly no purple pigment. Like the loaders of Noverca, they spoke among themselves using strange terms, such as someday, nowadays, tonight, evening, morning and last night, all-night and all-day. They said "birthday" instead of birthdate. The famous physics professor Boris

Darkwood also used these words in his lectures in the temple.

"But where to?" Elya asked.

"To Mrs Darkwood's. All our friends will gather there for the wake."

Elya felt completely cut off. Had he become a stranger? Not a friend? It was like he didn't know Harlow personally and hadn't visited their house. Even as Phoebe's study buddy when they took lessons from the holoprojector master together. She was much friendlier then. What had happened? Elya felt a demon rise in him with the name "Whim," as hot as boiling water. It demanded that Elya sulk, say something nasty, slam the door of the Bakers' vehicle and drive away on his conbike, swelling with resentment. But he had been taught to fight this demon from the cradle. Only at first glance did it seem a harmless whim, an emotional outburst. But you must not give in to it. It would make you say and do things you later regret for the rest of your life.

Elya took a deep breath, closed his eyes, and recited in his mind an ancient prayer that he once found in one of the earthly bibles.

"And to see you always from afar,
Follow your voice as you walk by,

But here I speak down to you.
And I never look you in the eye ..."

Something was not right here. If Phoebe didn't have feelings for him, she wouldn't have attended his lecture for schoolchildren at the museum last week. He just had to be patient, and then she would explain everything when the time came.

The whim stumbled, rolled into the darkest corner of consciousness, and melted there, leaving behind minor burns to Elya's pride. He sighed again and opened his eyes. Phoebe watched his face with curiosity, but then she frowned and turned away.

"Well then, see you when I see you," Elya said, as affably as possible, "and tell Groonya ..."

"Yes, I know." Phoebe waved at him and dug into the amulet that looked like a powder box.

Elya calmly got on his conbike and drove as slowly as possible towards the road to New Tokyo. After all, Viola – the architexter's secretary – had sent him the address and time of the commemoration.

6. Village

The most disagreeable role in the village was the janitor. Even low tide gatherers who picked snails in the coastal mud were more respected.

A young village woman named Melza was a typical young rehabilitated runaway. In her early teens she helped her mother at the farm with the cleaning and polishing. And she enjoyed doing it back there. She used to have robotic glass cleaners, remotely controlled scrubbers and vacuum cleaners built into the floor in every room. Even looking after the animals was fun for her.

Now she was scrubbing the floors in the Great Martyr's house, and she had to do it with a water bucket and a rag, as earthlings did in rough times. Like all the houses in the village, the Great Martyr's chambers were made of stone and clay but bigger, better on the inside, and furnished with things smuggled from the main colony. Melza recognised proper tables and chairs made of artificial materials, good fabric and even silver dining utensils. She could only guess how these things made their way outside the city borders.

In the camping tent that all exiles were allowed to bring from the city, she managed to camp only before arriving in the village. There, one of the guards immediately took it off her. Now Melza lived not in a house but under the rubble of a salt buoy. Sea creatures called blobsters made those spheres during their mating season and then discarded them. Many years ago, when the village's population was no more than fifty households, there were no stone houses here, and all the villagers lived in such hollow salt spheres. But now, these spheres were used for salting fish, and for storage, chicken coops and goat sheds. No one could tell her when and by what great force one ball had been split into pieces, but Melza could see it was cut in half with a fully charged zapper. The villagers made something like a canopy for the new girl from the largest piece- almost half the whitish sphere. They left it on the edge of the settlement, which was not even guarded by the usual village patrol. Living under the "hemisphere" – as Melza called it – was like living under an overturned boat, but it was reasonably dry and not as hot as in a grass hut.

She also had to do all the dirty work in the village, for which she was paid only with better food and old unwanted things. It was also impossible not to work as if she didn't do this, she wouldn't receive her share of the common harvest. Everything collected and prepared by the whole village in one cycle was brought to a large deck of stems in front of the martyr's house. The meat of the sea dwellers, fish, fresh eggs, roots, tocks, bread, goat's milk and herbs was first attended to by the martyr's cares, and the rest was divided among the other villagers. But although the rule was to split everything equally, Melza still got less than the others.

The girl deeply regretted that she had succumbed to the temptation for which she had to pay such a high price. However, until now, she hadn't been able to understand why her parents supported the rehabilitation order. She used to bite her lip in anger as she remembered her last conversation with her mother.

"I get punished for something as small as a box of candies? How is that fair? I can't believe you agreed with this?"

"First, not for candies, but for theft, which is unacceptable in our society. Second, four cycles of rehabilitation is not a punishment. It is an attempt to fix what is broken in your set of moral standards," the mother replied with pain in her voice. "And I had to agree because this is the penalty for me. I failed to teach you the importance of respecting principles."

Now it seemed to her that she didn't even remember the taste of toffees, but she suffered much more because now she had only two dresses, one pair of shoes and an old backpack. Everything else from the luggage brought with her from the city was immediately taken away by other villagers. They left her a toothbrush too, but without toothpaste. All other things in the village were shared, as were four other girls of the same age as Melza. All and sundry used them for a modest fee, but no one dared touch Melza.

Sometimes she wished they did, but she had a good reason for that. And not because of extra food, gifts or sweet bark. On the cycle of her arrival, she became terrified. All the village inhabitants looked similar because of the protective clay on their faces. She was brought to the Great Martyr Morbus Contagione, who examined and felt Melza, as if she were one of the goats brought for sale from a neighbouring village.

"Do not spoil this one on pain of death," the Great Martyr said, "I wish to save her for myself, for the times I returned what was stolen from me."

Since then, Melza lived in constant terror. She didn't understand why the martyr kept her safe, but this did not promise anything good. As she cleaned martyr's bedroom, Melza was careful not to touch the basket beside the large bed. The basket was covered with a dirty cloth. The smell from it was heart-rending. She guessed what was stored in it, but the martyr didn't give the order, and Melza didn't volunteer to get rid of it.

This powerful village leader often silently and closely watched Melza as she cleaned the house. The martyr's long and thin fingers with iron rings slowly scratched their own bony purple shoulder. And their watery eyes followed Melza's every move. It was very unsettling. The girl was unsure what she hated more, that hungry stare or her job. But that was it. Morbus never sent for Melza or allowed others to approach her. Because of such a privilege, others disliked her, and making friends with other people of all genders was impossible. No other villager escaped being called at least once into Morbus's bedroom, and each villager's screams terrified those who could hear them. It was called "receiving the blessing" or "sharing the martyr's burden," depending on how long they spent in the holy chambers and in what condition they returned. A couple of people returned dead because they failed to honour the Lord's wish.

Of course, the villagers didn't worship O'Teka as they worshipped the Lord. In the village, no one prayed to the Lord. They only begged him for mercy and fortune. And since the Lord hears the prayers of the sufferers better, Morbus usually did the begging on behalf of his fellow villagers. And they had to show gratitude.

Melza missed praying, but it was forbidden, and there were no bibles anyway. Not even a single leaflet. Actually, no ... not true. Some words were written on thick dry leaves of a vablish plant in the back room to the martyr's chamber. Melza suspected she was the only one who knew about them as she passed that room during her work, but when she glanced at those words, she didn't see much. The leaves were in typical black, but the ink was made from local glowing fungi and could be seen only in the dark. She couldn't look closely, being under constant scrutiny.

Melza once also saw something forbidden for ordinary villagers – dissembled electronic equipment. Melza was never good at school, and technology wasn't her passion; moreover, she was unsure what was. But she was dying of curiosity and wondered what Morbus was doing with all that.

One cycle, when she finished cleaning, the Great Martyr asked Melza if she minded helping them all out. She got very scared, but Morbus told her to open her mouth and placed a small flake of sweet bark on her tongue.

"I will give you a handful if you help me with my experiment and keep quiet about it," said Morbus and smiled pleasantly.

She agreed, followed Morbus to the secret room, and the next thing she knew, she was standing in the woods far away from the village.

She felt cold, and her feet were covered in stone cuts, blood and dirt. Her head ached mercilessly, but the fright overpowered the pain. She screamed and almost fainted but noticed the boarding posts that separated the civilised colony from the wild lands. Two people were standing there, talking quietly. One was a fellow villager called Gafan, and the other was a woman dressed as a farmer. Between them, there was a small but full sack on the grass. She heard them talking.

"See? It works," said Gafan.

"Hmm. I'm impressed. But how do you think I shall conceal it from the ordermen in the city?" said the woman, picking the sack up. "And how did

Contagione manage to avoid our scanning detectors?"

"Do you know what this blue stuff is?" Gafan asked.

"Not really."

"Neither do I, but it seems to jam the scanners. You just have to get creative and make it into something less suspicious-looking."

"Okay, I will look into it. If it works, don't worry about the payment. But if it doesn't, and I get discovered, I will take you all down with me. How many of these were made?"

"I don't know. More than one but at the testing stage. None are ready for the temple yet."

The woman nodded, restored the power border, and walked away, disappearing into the darkness of the woods. Gafan approached Melza, who hugged herself to warm up, although it wasn't cold in this region.

"What's happening?" she asked, but Gafan laughed.

"Magic! Let's get back," he said and started towards the road.

Four cycles later, a rumour spread through the village about a fire in the colony. And not just anywhere but in White Capital. The villagers joked and sneered about this, but Melza didn't rejoice with the rest. She somehow felt that she was involved in this fire. However, she couldn't figure out how.

She longed for city life and wanted to belong to a colony and not a village full of god-believing mystics. However, it was still too early for her to make a decision or hope to return.

7. The Commemoration

Elya was surprised that there weren't too many people in Dr Zina's house, but everyone was talking about Harlow all cycle.

Despite both being nordians, Harlow and Scarlett didn't often spend time at their clan's family gatherings. Only Harlow's parents and a dozen of Scarlett's siblings came to the wake. Da Costa had married and lived for some time in Carib, on the island of Pettogreco, where most of the population were earthlings – settlers from the second wave. But after they decided to have a couple of babies – cloned according to the ninth-century method – the couple unexpectedly arrived in Altyn District and told old Baker, the former master of Harlow, that they wanted to start their own farm in the white-walled capital. Both pregnant, round, cute and shaggy, they looked very enthusiastic and happy.

"They thought I was messing with them and rolled with laughter when I asked, 'and which of you was my apprentice?' But I really wasn't sure. Was it so hard to shave before such an important appointment?" Rod Baker said from his wheelchair. His hand, holding a glass of wine, trembled slightly.

"You just became blind in your old age, Rod," said a plump Black woman with a French accent and a long, thick, almost white braid. "Scarlett's hair is much redder, isn't it?"

She put her arms around the widow, who sat like a frozen stone. Scarlett was combed and dressed in mourning colours. Her head was slightly tilted to one side, and all cycle she politely nodded her thanks to everyone who expressed condolences. But her eyes were dead. Her daughter Zinaida, named after Mrs Darkwood, and son Thomas, named after Captain Darkwood, had already been dragged into the garden by nordian relatives. From the green labyrinth, loud exclamations and verses of some northern hymn were heard every now and then.

The remnants of the former crew of the famous *Wasp* ship sat on cushions scattered across the floor in Mrs Darkwood's fashionable Samarkandian room. In addition to them, the Baker sisters, Elya, and a handsome, ageing woman named Matilda also were in the room. She held Scarlett's hand and didn't say a word. Occasionally, she glanced at the low-level loader present – Steven McLeod – an Australian of German-Scottish origin with thinning blond hair but still handsome and strong. It is said there was once something between them.

"Zina, do you have a vacancy for Scarlett in the hospital?" Steven McLeod asked, "She was your best assistant, and Rod is sure that the factory can't be restored any time soon."

The Black woman looked inquiringly into Scarlett's face, but it didn't change. Rod Baker sipped his wine and nodded.

"Jaxon says he'll take care of the rescued eggs and larvae, and he will owe you. Think about it, Scarlett, my dear."

"What about Phoebe? She's been our apprentice for six months now." Scarlett's face brightened for a moment.

"Don't worry about me, Master Da Costa," Phoebe said, sitting to her father's left, "My purpose will still be in communications. I just wanted to do something nice for Dad, so I could talk to him about bugs and tease Jaxon."

"Phoebe, you are a terrible hypocrite," said Groonya, seated to her father's right, with a snort.

"Rod, how did you figure that out?" came a voice from the room's darkest corner. General King was twirling an empty glass in his hands, settled on a high stool. "If we all chip in, we can rebuild the factory in less than a year."

Without looking at him, Rod Baker nodded and said, "If we can make it in time for the next sandies' mating season. Instead of larvae, Jaxon will repay the debt with adults and then—"

"That's for Scarlett to decide when she feels better," the voice with metallic undertones said in a softer and more feminine tone than usual.

The architexter handed the glass to Master McLeod, who topped it up with a garnet-coloured wine, almost brown in the light of the white lamps.

Then Steven McLeod turned to the widow, "Scarlet, baby, just say the word. We won't let you down."

"Vist, we can clear it all out and get the site ready in less than a week," said Mik King.

"I know, but that's not the problem? I still need to analyse samples from the conflagration before you start destroying the evidence."

"Destroying what?" Dr Zina raised her eyebrows.

Vist shook their head. "Guys, are you completely colonials now? I understand that today is about the memory of Harlow, and we all want to help Scarlett, but ... Mik, even you don't mind the fact that it was arson. Don't you want to know who did it and why?"

The corner where Mik King sat seemed to get even darker. His amulet was a circlet on a smoothly shaved head.

"To be honest, I am more interested in 'who.' My guys collected everything you asked for, Architexter. You will take care of 'why,' I am sure."

"Very good." Vist put her glass on the floor. "The worst thing that happened after the last forced expulsion from the colony was the fight between the fans for the Obsidian and Orbit teams, which ended in an early rehabilitation. Arson has always been considered an unacceptable law violation both on Earth and on Noverca. It just hasn't happened here for generations. Even the Grand has not yet contacted me with the right questions. General, did he contact you?"

"No." The whites of Mik King's eyes flashed unkindly.

"The Grand has sent me his formal condolences," said Scarlett tearfully, pushing away Matilda's fingers and covering her face with her hands – they looked as if she were wearing fluffy gloves.

Vist got up and paced the room. "The fire was not accidental and must be investigated. Mik, arsonists are not a team of brawlers. They won't come to you with a confession, having sobered up the next morning. We've lived here too long, and we've begun to forget."

"Vist! Today is a bad time for—" Steven McLeod said.

Scarlett took her hands away from her face, and it lit up with a blush on her shaved cheeks for the first time that cycle. "No, no. It's a good time. Your last investigation turned out to be so fateful for me. I met Harlow. Master Architexter, you are absolutely right. Please find the one who burned my life and took away my love."

"I promise you, Scarlett, I will do it." Vist's voice hardened and lowered with every word. "But I will need help. I will need our medics' skill and experience and our scouts' strength and agility. I will need the engineering craft of an inventor and the swiftness of young feet."

Elya knew that about a generation ago, this team finished looking for lost evacuation pods, and the life of the adventure was as tempting now as it could be. The shared memories thickened and electrified the air in the room. Everyone present looked at each other. Vist settled back into a comfortable position and grinned through his white teeth.

Mik King got up, walked out of the dark corner, and sat next to Vist on the carpet. Rod Baker shot his eyes across their faces and smirked. Steven McLeod clenched his fists and grinned too. Since many were already sitting on the carpet, they all seemed to Elya to be children who gathered in a circle on the floor for an exciting game. Matilda stepped back from Scarlett and pressed her fingers to her temples. Phoebe and Groonya watched all this with amazement, and Elya, sitting quietly next to Phoebe, regretted that he had not been born fifty years ago.

"Didn't you notice anything strange painted on the factory's wall?" Vist asked, but no one had time to answer.

One of the thin walls slid aside. A grey-haired and strong earthling named Nathaniel Alloway entered the room with his wife Andrea, followed by a very tall and thin loader named Obydva.

"Sorry, we're late," said Nathaniel. "Obydva brought so much food; we spent ages unpacking it for you."

In the hands of his wife, a huge bouquet of white lilies sparkled like earthly snow. Scarlett stood up and embraced all the newly arrived, who had to bow to her level. Obydva stared at Rod, Phoebe and Groonya with an incredible expression.

"It's time to go home," Rod Baker said softly to his daughters, lowering his head.

Groonya quickly got up, grabbed the handles of her father's wheelchair, and promptly took him out of the room into the garden. Phoebe whispered a few apologies into Scarlett's ear and then followed her sister. Elya gathered all his will into a knot and ... stayed put.

Good thing he did.

After a while, the conversation about arson was resumed.

"The ordermen do not really know how to do this," said Mik King. "They are all young, and for them, this duty service is mostly boring and therefore is only a temporary career."

"Of course," Steven McLeod said, sighing. "Kids like the order-uniform. The schoolchildren vilifying it for several years was the main reason for your success."

General King shook his head. "Don't say that. Despite different future careers, they receive good, ongoing physical training and appreciate this duty's importance. Having served the due time conscientiously and honestly, for the most part, only then do they turn down the officer job vacancy, if there is one, to quit and choose another purpose, having already proven their capability to themselves at least."

"And then many of them join our academy and become scouts," Steven McLeod said, nodding.

Matilda didn't take her eyes off him. In a languid voice she said, "Steven, why don't your scouts have such beautiful uniforms?"

"Because there is no need for it in fieldwork," McLeod replied, sounding slightly annoyed. "The shiny buttons will attract all sorts of svoloch."

"Then maybe the scouts need to look for arsonists?" Nathaniel asked. "Steven and I can select the right people."

"Work in the city should still be done by ordermen," Mik replied. It is their duty. I regret that I didn't create an investigative group. Even just in case."

"Once upon a time on Earth, just in case, we created entire armies," Obydva said thoughtfully, "and they came in handy in the end."

Vist turned to Obydva and asked in his usual metallic undertone, "My friend, have you left Pettogreco for a long time?"

"For a few cycles, most likely. I need to talk to you."

Obydva tilted his head, which Elya understood as "alone," but he was unsure.

"We will talk, but I have a suggestion to all," Vist said to everyone. "There is a lot of material in the temple's archives of earthly literature about how intentional violations of the social behaviour's conduct were previously investigated. In the history of Earth, they were not just frequent but very regular and were also called crimes. Moreover, ignorance of the law did not exempt the criminal from punishment. Here, people make random mistakes, and there have been no intentional killings for many years. Many violations in our colony were committed by earthlings of the last resettlement and sectarians living outside the colony."

"But it was impossible to call their actions a trifle. They didn't accept the ways of the colony. The last case here was a massacre with cannibalism and fraud of incredible proportions," Obydva said without emotion.

Elya noticed Steven McLeod wince and run his hand over his thigh as if in pain.

"Mik, Steven, Obydva, Nat," Vist said. "I invite you to become members of a small detective agency, to which I summon you as investigators and operatives. Your implants can come in handy if you have to work outside the colony, and you can enlist your trusted ordermen and scout cadets to help."

The ex-Earth marines and pilots looked pleased with the offer, and McLeod even punched Mik King in the shoulder while Nat Alloway whistled.

"And I couldn't even hope—"

Vist continued. "Zina and Scarlett, I hope you will agree to work as my forensic scientists, and Mrs Alloway ... I have a special task for you. Our former ship engineer, Rod Baker, turned down my offer to load him and became a very feeble elder. Your engineering excellence and great ideas might—"

"She agrees! Isn't it right, darling?" Nathaniel said.

Andrea Alloway nodded, "Of course, but how you can be sure that your search will go beyond the colony's borders?"

Vist replied, "I am not sure of anything. At least for now. Like Mik said – just in case. My instinct tells me that something is starting, and we will all have to work hard soon. This arson was a warning with the intention to hurt, to upset. There was something personal in it! I want to be ready for anything."

"And I? Can I be of help?" asked Matilda from a quiet corner. She looked almost pleadingly at the loader.

Master Steven glared at Vist and gave a barely perceptible "no."

"If you can, Miss Crossich, I will definitely come to you," Vist answered quite frankly.

"I can't help," said Scarlett suddenly. "Can you do it without me this time? I am not quite myself recently."

"But, my dear!" Dr Zina hugged Scarlett by the shoulders with one arm. "It would be so good for you."

"No," the widow got up and went to the exit so as not to burst into tears again in front of everyone. "Forgive me. Please, Tilda, will you help me see my relatives out? They were so noisy."

"Of course."

It was evident that Matilda didn't want to leave, but she couldn't help but follow Scarlett.

Everyone in the room was silent for a while, and then they too noticed that Vist was looking at Elya. Everyone turned their heads to him, and Elya thought his hair would flare up on his head.

He swallowed and said in a voice hoarse with excitement, "Mrs Alloway, I beg you to accept me as your apprentice."

"Who is this?" Obydva asked Nathaniel quietly.

"Rod's future son-in-law, as far as I know," Nat replied in the same whisper.

But Elya, with his Uzhan's ear, heard these words and squared his shoulders.

8. In the Boat

The low tide exposed the top of a small island. There was nothing there, just a few shells and crabs, but unlike the dinghy, it kept still and was better suited for communication.

After the ritual on the wet sand, the two women returned to the boat. The farmer called Karlina resumed rowing and told her guest how she managed to fool the sea guards. But the guest wrapped herself more tightly in a yellow shawl and looked suspiciously around and at the waves.

"Karlina, you told me there are no settlements here," she said in a rough voice, frowning.

"There aren't. No one comes here except other boats. Fishermen do not claim these waters much. Scientists come for samples once a month."

"Then who is that?"

Karlina peered into the thickness of the green water and saw a whitish human silhouette about three metres beneath the surface. A perfect female figure swam away from under the hull of their boat towards the horizon.

"That's the ikhtee," Karlina said. "They live in an underwater city south of here. I rarely see them in the capital. They sell delicacies mined from the seabed and trinkets made from corals and mother-of-pearl. This one would have already surfaced and started talking if she was interested in us. I think she's going about her own business."

"She saw us. How can we get rid of her?"

"We just have to wait. It doesn't look like this one is coming back."

The guest didn't answer but started scratching her shoulder. There was nothing wrong with it, but a habit is a habit. The farmer grimaced in displeasure.

"Stop doing that. Matilda will moan for hours until the skin you scratched heals."

The woman in the yellow shawl sneered but folded her hands in her lap and peered overboard again.

"It looks like we're alone now. Show me where this place is."

A few minutes later, two women in the boat left the grey sand of the small island far behind.

"So, why exactly do they visit this place?" The woman turned to the farmer again.

"The wild ones never go as far as that island. They would be easily seen there from the shore. They only reach the middle of this chain of rocks during the migration season. There is a place where at low tide, a shallow depression is formed. It is rich in small marine life, renewed with each high tide. Local fishermen know about it but are also aware of the competition. Therefore during the migration of the wild ones, they do not show their noses here at all."

The boat sailed for another few hundred metres by a series of sharp, toothlike rocks.

"Is this the spot?" the guest soon asked.

"Yes. For the last time, please stop scratching!"

"You will place it here. This location is good enough for my control of that border. I'll give you a more advanced device for city work."

"I don't have any more blue salt."

"Salt will come too. The wild ones will gather it for me in the northern caves. One last thing: Matilda works too slowly. Do you want your daughter to stay safe and sound?"

"Yes."

"Then make sure she memorise everything she learns about what is in the architexter's house when I am not with her. Until next time." With those last words, the woman fell back, rolled her eyes, and groaned.

Karlina rushed to her and put her hand under her shoulders and head.

"Matilda! My girl, are you all right?"

The voice that answered her was feeble and not as rough as a minute ago.

"Mum, I can't take it any more. That svoloch scratched me to pieces again."

"And there will be no more of it. Enough is enough!"

Karlina carefully washed Matilda's shoulders with seawater and covered her with a shawl.

"Here you are! It was not that long this time. We will head home in just a minute."

After making her daughter comfortable in the boat, the farmer rowed to the nearest rock. There, she picked up a small oblong object from under her seat and wrapped it in the baby blanket. Standing up to her full height, Karlina lowered the bundle into a wide crack in the black rock. It stuck in it like a wedge, and now only its top was visible, and only from the western side.

Then Karlina folded the oars, started the ZPE-motor, and headed towards the port.

9. The Assassin

Well, fancy that! What a surprise! The target took the bait and turned up.

And they say this is the smartest person on the planet.

A figure in a dark robe stepped out of the four-seater conmot. The hot wind immediately lifted the long copper hair off one side. The person in the robe walked a few steps forwards and stopped at a wide shield with a coast map. It appeared as if he ... or she ... was looking for something.

In the dense shade under the black foliage, the sniper sat down with his feet in the target's direction, resting his toes on the stone ledges. He carefully put both feet into the piercer's stirrups, pulled the bowstring towards his chin, and slowly lay down on his back.

He squinted at the tiny weather display showing the strength and direction of the wind, aimed at the person's head, and made appropriate adjustments.

In the last forty-six years, he had never missed a hunt. Never!

He focused for a second on the tip of the screw arrow and imagined it taking all the ancient technology out of that skull, along with the loader's brains. The sniper shifted his eyes to the reddish hair a couple of hundred metres before him and unclenched his fingers.

He thought the loader jerked, but the sound of the arrow hitting the shield was not what he expected. The map's holo-screen flickered and went out, and the target stood as if nothing had happened nearby and then looked towards the bay.

It's impossible. For forty-six years ... not once!

"Don't be too upset, buddy," a voice very close by said. "It wasn't a miss. Believe me, I know. I used to be a hunter myself once upon a time. Vist heard every move of yours, pulse and breathing included. But sixteen years ago, even they would not have had time to dodge from such a short distance. It's a gene – a gift from an old friend. Loaders are almost as agile as the svoloch nowadays."

With these words, a completely grey-haired but strong earthling pulled the trigger, and the bewildered hunter felt as if his body was swaddled in a tight knot. He could not move a finger or tongue and only stared in horror at the man with the immobiliser on his right knuckle. The man effortlessly picked up and threw the assassin over his left shoulder. With the other hand, he grabbed the piercer and walked towards the destroyed map stand.

"I hope you have enough funds to repair the damage to the colony," he said and pushed the prisoner into the back seat of the conmot. He folded the piercer and hung it on his back.

The confused hunter realised that his attempt made no impression on the temple of O'Teka's architexter. From the back of the conmot, he saw the grey-haired man walk up to the loader and silently stand beside him. Or her. Salt spheres of various sizes were scattered along the shore of the bay. About a dozen were still rocking in the green sea waves.

"Nat," the sniper finally heard a low voice with a metallic undertone say, "this is the very bay in which we first saw the blobster buoys when we landed on Noverca for the first time. I wouldn't even have remembered if the holoshield's info hadn't pointed to this 'historical fact.' Is it really that interesting for visitors to the bay?"

An Earthman picked up three whitish spheres the size of a tennis ball from the sand and playfully but skilfully juggled them. "Of course, it's interesting. I was not with you at that time, but it was here that I arranged the first date with Andrea. She was delighted with the spectacle. It was the blobsters' mating season, and we were fortunate with the weather."

"How fast time flies! There are so few of us left from that group. Chang and Général were still alive on that trip. Tolyan and Marta were two different people. Tom was still with us. And how young was Rod! Harlow hadn't even been born yet."

Nat lowered his hands, and two spheres fell to the ground. "I'm sorry, Architexter. We'll all miss her."

"Time to go."

The loader sighed, glanced at the piercer that nearly ended their life, and wandered back.

The sniper noticed the clouds had thinned. In Vitr's pinkish light, the off-white salt spheres turned a peachy pink with an unpleasant tinge. The smallest ones crunched under the loader's feet. The Earthman threw the third sphere into the sea waves, returned, and took the driving seat.

* * *

On the way to the city, Nat asked, "Vist, how did you know about the ambush and assassination attempt?"

"There was no way for me to know. It was simply the most reasonable thing to assume that if the factory burning was an arson attack, and these coordinates were left there intentionally – then they were a message from an arsonist. The clumsy doodle of five fingers I misinterpreted. It looked like a glove, but my hopes that this was a challenge to a duel didn't materialise."

"And why did you decide they were left just for you?"

"You were at the scene of the fire. Did you see it?"

"No ... I saw a wall. And doodles too. I mistook it for old graffiti."

"No one saw it. The one who left it there was sure I would spot the doodles and understand them."

"So he knows you well enough." Nat grinned and turned onto the main road, which was denser and drier.

"Too well."

"But this assassin; he doesn't look like an expert in loaders."

"You couldn't expect a loader expert to come and try to kill me himself. Frankly, the best options would have been a duel, or at least a conversation with him, but the chances of those were microscopic."

"And who do you think sent this shooter after you?"

"I don't know."

"But you suspect someone."

"It's too early to suspect anyone. But you can speculate."

Nat perked up. He loved those kinds of conversations with his former mentor. Vist surely knows how to reason. Nat glanced back to the subdued prisoner and lowered his voice, "Then the first question is – why in the bay? Besides the fact that it's a famous spot and there are places to hide."

Vist didn't have to whisper. Their fingers touched the smooth throat, and Nat heard a metallic voice right in his left ear, where he had an implant the size of a rice grain, "Interesting. Well? Go on."

The loader's lips moved, but the prisoner could not see them from the back seat.

Nat continued quietly. "Judging by his weapons and clothes, this hunter is not a city dweller. He obviously lives in one of the exiled villages. And even if he could infiltrate the city, his piercer would attract much unwanted attention."

"I agree. Finding such a person in the villages is easier than in the civil zone. Does this mean that his employer is in the wildlands too?"

"Not at all," Nat replied. "There have been cases in the past. In the city, it is easier for your killer to get lost."

"Are there other reasons for this conclusion?"

"The city dweller has more funds to pay for the job done?"

"Right. I can guess with which currency. Did you notice anything special on the piercer's body?"

Nat stopped the conmot, threw his hand behind his neck, and pulled the weapon from his back by the strap. He examined the metal arc carefully and noticed a flat nozzle at the very end. "An amulet?"

"No. We would have sensed it. It has no communication with the temple, only with the satellite. I bet this is a simple tool for navigation and aiming."

"A weather band? Only those who work in the fields and farms are equipped with such devices. But he could have stolen it from the scouts."

"Could have. Wait, I won't be long."

Vist's eyes closed for a few minutes, and Nat drove on.

Soon Nate heard Vist again. "Since the scouts began using weather bands, there has not been a single loss of such an instrument registered in the temple archives. But here, I don't have access to the most recent reports. I'll check them out when we get home."

"What if it's not there?"

"So it was obtained in the capital. Then the chance will be higher that the buyer is there."

"This means nothing ... but never mind. We'll arrive soon, and this fellow will tell us everything."

The remains of the old city wall looked white from a distance, but close up, it became clear they were decorated with pieces of salt sphere, like convex tiles. Since the white-walled capital had become almost three times as large as before, the old wall had lost its role as a reflector and barrier and had been dismantled. As a memorial to it, a piece of the old city gate made from the cargo hatch of *Noah-8*, the spaceship the first colonists arrived on, stood there. The quarantine building with showers and cleansers was also no longer needed.

They arrived under the capital's protective dome and drove along the neutraliser's corridor, where radioactive particles were blown off them, and then drove out onto the city's streets. Nat dropped the architexter off near the temple and then turned towards Kinghall.

"I'll join you in an hour. I also have a few questions for him," Nat heard Vist say in the earpiece, and he nodded to the loader through the window.

And indeed, exactly fifty-eight minutes later, the hired killer turned his eyes from Vist to Nat and back. He was now immobilised just below the waist and sat in a special chair. There was no fear in his eyes but rather mockery. Vist didn't report to Nat what they did during those minutes. Nat was already used to it, knowing that important things would not be hidden from him. He asked the first question, which made the captive's smile disappear. "Citizens are expelled from civilised cities for violating the law. Do you know where exiles who break the law are driven out to? Have you ever met any svoloch?"

The prisoner swallowed nervously and said, "I have never heard of such a thing ... It would be tantamount to murder. Colonists don't execute—"

"You said the same words almost fifty years ago when you were expelled after the rehabilitation expired. But you didn't die, although you were not even twenty years old. Maybe now you will survive ... in the mountains."

The prisoner cringed. "I wasn't expelled. I left."

"All the same. Your name then was Christover Ahiga. What is your name now?"

"Just Ahiga."

"And why? Have you lost your individuality, or do you now represent your entire bloodline?"

"What consequences do you fear more? Capital court or retribution for a failed assassination attempt?"

Ahiga scratched his purple ear and dropped his hands on his knees, saying, "You still won't believe me. You paralysed me with your gadget, but my client used something much worse on me. Oh, what is there to say? It's useless."

"Just try." Nat looked back at Vist and said, "Why don't I bring us all some refreshments?"

"And for our guest, too, while he decides."

Nat left through a door transparent from the outside only, and he observed what would happen next. Vist stood before the prisoner and gazed at his face with unblinking eyes. And when Ahiga's expression changed as if he started to remember something, Vist quickly stepped towards him and placed their open hand on the prisoner's balding forehead.

10. Phoebe

"Hi, may I come in?"

"Papa!"

Phoebe rushed through the spice garden and threw her arms around Obydva's skinny neck. They were almost the same height.

The loader embraced Phoebe by pressing his hands gently at first and then firmly on her back. He closed his eyes, inhaled the scent of the girl's hair, and said, "You still use pine shampoo."

"Yes, Papa. And you still burn saxaul when cooking baranimal kebab."

"Only on special occasions. For weddings, anniversaries … and funerals."

They froze in a brief embrace and then let go of each other.

Phoebe smiled. "I couldn't believe my eyes when you walked in today amid the wake."

Obydva shifted his gaze from the beaming Phoebe to Groonya's gloomy face, who stood by the water barrel.

Groonya approached Obydva in response to his look. "If you're here to see Dad, you may have wasted your time."

"I'm seeing you two now, aren't I? So that time is well spent. I'm glad I came. That wasn't easy."

Groonya's eyes filled with tears, and she hugged Obydva. "I miss you so much!" she whispered.

"You squint like Marta," an old, grumpy voice from the front door said. "And your gait is like hers ... elegant and silent."

Rod removed his hands from the wheels of his chair and clasped his fingers over the blanket.

"I can still stomp like a behemoth if you like," said Obydva.

"Please don't. My bloody head will ache. Well, you look terrible. You've become so bony and ... too serious."

"And you are so old."

"Ha! And you are still such a pillock." Rod's dark lips stretched into a smile.

The girls looked at each other with wide eyes. Groonya nodded slightly towards the gate, and Phoebe blinked at her in agreement. They moved like the wind; they disappeared from the garden, stopped at the street corner, and both exhaled.

"Phew, I thought I would get hysterical," said Groonya.

"I know … Isn't it crazy? How long was it?"

"Not sure. Twenty-six years? Twenty-eight?"

"Something like that."

Groonya looked back and peered into the thickets of sea-buckthorn. "They went in … they're finally talking. We should give them some space, but what are we going to do for now?"

Phoebe thought about it, looked back at the mansion, and then gazed into the distance at the narrow strip of spire above it. "We can go to the temple and pray a little. Finally, you can download materials on ancient Earth poetry and some romance novels."

"No, you go. I'm staying here in case Dad has a seizure. You never know what to expect from, well, both of them."

"I'm glad you didn't say 'all three' this time."

"Perhaps I should have. Go. I'll beacon you if need be."

"But you were going to meet with Jaxon before the end of the cycle."

"Well, I will see him another time. He will wait."

"Ah, Groonya, watch it. One day he will stop waiting for you."

"I know. Go and have a good time."

Groonya placed her hand on her sister's shoulder for a second, returned to the house, and settled on a bench under the roses by the front door. She removed the amulet from her wrist and waved at Phoebe. "Go, go!"

Phoebe pasted the house and walked down the street.

She noticed a familiar figure at the fountain on the way to the square. It was an old acquaintance, Matilda Crossich. Phoebe was about to greet her when she noticed something odd about the woman's posture. She seemed to be talking to someone, but Phoebe couldn't see anyone near her or a holo-screen. She supposed the woman was on an audio call, but then Matilda raised her hand and pointed angrily at the temple.

"There!" Phoebe heard an exclamation. "Where else? Stupid!"

She felt embarrassed, as if she were eavesdropping on someone's conversation. She raised her hand, called to Matilda, and went straight across the street towards her. Matilda turned with an inhuman expression, but it immediately changed, and a beautiful smile returned as if nothing had happened.

"Miss Baker!" said a pleasant voice without a trace of irritation, "What a surprise! Are you off to the temple?"

"Yes. I need to kill a couple of hours."

"Is that so? Got extra time, ha? That isn't like you at all. But again, your factory is no more ..." Matilda said, then her eyes suddenly shone, "Would you mind doing me a little favour then? I really need to find a suitable seascape to project onto the wall in my new room. You have a better taste. As you know, mine is not the most artistic one in the whole colony. Help me capture something really beautiful on the southeast beach. Pretty please."

"Where the yellow rocks are? Forty minutes' walk from here, behind the city walls?"

"That's right."

"Very well, let's go then. If you're lucky, there will be clouds!"

"Excellent."

The two women slowly walked towards the east gate, talking in a friendly manner. No one saw them again that cycle.

11. The Architexter

Nat and Vist approached the architexter's house roughly when Mik and Steven arrived at its gate. All four entered and went through the hall and into the back garden towards the tea pavilion.

Vist's garden was not the largest in the colony, but there were more flowers, pergolas and greenhouses than in the city park, Paradise. It was built both below the floor and above on several platforms. So the garden was as high as the mansion itself. Or rather, it was part of the house. The biggest part.

Like everything in the mansion, this garden was the work and design of the architexter. A cloned margay modified for the lack of darkness was sleeping under an olive tree. From low trees on the upper platforms, the white and lilac petals of the *aeternum cerasus*, or the eternal cherry, fell down on the grass all year round and were immediately carried off by large white ants. Butterflies of all sizes and colours fluttered around. Vist bred insects and plants specifically for this garden, but Grand willingly bought larvae and seedlings for the city, like the loader's other creations and works of art.

"You're both alive. I guess that's the good news for this cycle," said Steven instead of a greeting.

"I'll tell you what the good news is," Mik said. "We built a team of thirty men and women to form the new squad. We called it Law Force, and it will be able to work both in and outside the colony. They prefer to call themselves coppers, and I suspect Steven and Rod have something to do with that."

Steven grimaced. "Why am I immediately involved? Ask the government. They have been raving recently about the history of the Earth police. The Grand wanted to hold dedication ceremonies and stuff like that. But we let them do it without us."

"But the best news," Nat said, pulling the chairs out, "is what Vist managed to extract from the assassin's head! Mik, now he is a first suspect and is all yours, and the new Law Force can deal with him. We left him in the Kinghall, ready to be charged."

Mik turned to Vist. "But to what end? For this assassination attempt, there can be no hearing. He is not a citizen, for a start. And he was not caught in the colony territory. He is not a spy. He is going straight back out."

"What? No retribution?" Steven sounded disappointed.

Vist ordered Viola to bring some tea and coffee and then said, "Apart from his attempt to kill a colonist, you will charge him with obtaining illegal electronic equipment, participating in smuggling, and damaging colony property. All his gear has been confiscated, which is this man's serious punishment. I am sure he would prefer to be dropped in the middle of a goon-fly nest."

A hatch opened in the middle of a large round table, and a tray full of cups, teapots and coffee pots rose from the well inside it.

"What about the arson?" asked Mik and took his favourite black mug from the tray.

"He knows nothing about it, unlike his client. This man was working for someone." Vist poured green tea from the transparent teapot. "Just like the person who burned the factory. Since the graffiti on the wall links them, they could be working for the same employer."

"A conspiracy!" Steven dropped two lumps of sugar into his coffee. "Tell us more."

"Well, he is not good at thinking straight, so all I got were blurry images and incomplete sentences. First, he thought of the village. I am not sure which one. But then I picked up a feeling. It was a very strong fear. He was very afraid of something ... or someone. He pictured something at the same time. It looked rather ... hmm. Let me project it for you."

Vist activated the screen right above the plate of cakes, and everyone saw a strange dark object like seven translucent bluish crystals stacked on top of each other. It started at the bottom with a hexagonal and a pentagonal prism, then there was a cube, then a ball, a cylinder and a dodecahedron with a cone at the very top. All the shapes were roughly the same size, but the size of the actual structure was hard to estimate, as it was taken from a memory or a dream.

"What the hell is that?" Steven asked.

"I don't know yet," Vist shrugged, "I haven't seen it before."

"Some sick religious artefact those villagers are so fond of," Nat said. "Like an idol ... or a totem."

"A new godly deity?" Steven said. "It resembles a man in a pointy hat."

"A legendary wizard then," Nat said with a grin. "I wonder if this deity is as tall as Obydva."

"Most likely, this thing is about the size of a bottle of uzhanian brandy," Steven said.

Mik grumbled. "I don't drink brandy and have no idea."

Steven said, "It could have been the size of your—"

"Guys, does it matter?" Vist said. "I am more fascinated in how the villagers, without our tools, could cut almost perfect geometrical shapes, most likely out of ..." – Vist blinked a few times – "an apparently blue salt; an impure mineral with a high percentage of algae dyes and mica."

Vist blinked and their olive eyes focused on the three men once again.

Mik put the empty mug on the table and said, "Now that is a scary thought, but I bet something about this idol frightened our villagers."

"Yes, and there is something else. His weather band was not purchased. It was part of the payment for his service. An advance. Had he succeeded he would have received a whole functional zapper as well. It wasn't a wish. He was pretty sure about it."

"No way. So there has to be someone in the colony who supplies technology to the banished ones." Nat got up and took a deep breath. "How are we going to find them?"

"The assassin does not know how the band came to the village, but the device itself can give us a clue. Please ask Andrea to analyse the band for me and establish the time and place of its production?" Vist then turned to Steven. "Your scouts in the geological department have a compound tracer, am I right?"

"Of course."

"Can we borrow it? There are substances in the blue salt that are not common in these parts. Blue salt can only be found in the north, although some of its components are in simple sea sand."

"I seem to understand your train of thought, architexter."

Vist continued. "Mik, how can we make our towns more vigilant?"

"For any suspicious activity, I can instruct my men to patrol the streets, like we did in our case with the environmentalists. We can activate the cameras with a recognition program if you have a face in mind. We also have bad-intention detectors, but they all need an upgrade, as they get a bit confused near the temple with people reading fiction in the bible hall."

Vist nodded and Nat asked, "Well, what do you want me to do after I have spoken to Andrea?"

Vist turned to him.

"Master Architexter." Viola's voice filled the room, "My brother Cesario in the temple urgently requires your presence. There was a security breach."

"Wow," Steven said, "looks like someone doesn't want to give us a break."

"Thank you, Viola. Tell him I am on my way." Vist got up. "Nat, please meet me later in the Waterfall Park in Altyn District. I will let you know the time."

"Sure."

"Do you need any help?" Mik asked.

"Not yet. I have a couple of temple guards there any way, so let me check it out first. You are going to be pretty busy today."

12. Melza

This cycle, the weekly begging began with a story from some ancient bible, not a song. This happened sometimes, and Melza immediately decided that she could try and sneak out of the assembly yard because the readings were not so noisy. The armed men, who stood guard throughout the village for hours, used it as an opportunity to nap.

One of the knitters once said that this martyr knows several Earth languages, and none of his grandfathers had ever heard such detailed stories. They are said to be even older than the vaults of O'Teka, and, therefore, they have to be purer and truer.

Melza had doubts about this even during her very first active role in the meeting. The story read or retold by the martyr was about a man on Earth who died a terrible and painful death to prove his faith in the Lord. Melza didn't remember his name, only that he was a hero and did the right thing. Then there was a story about how some people killed others for not believing strongly enough or for believing incorrectly. They, too, were right to do so, but Melza couldn't figure out what the others were doing to deserve death. Either they sang the anthem to the wrong tune, ate the wrong food, or did any of that at the wrong time. Then there was a story about a woman living in seclusion instead of sharing a home with her family. She did it for the love of God, and therefore it was right. Melza couldn't understand how this woman's relatives interfered with God and how the Lord allowed any men to father children while this was a sin for single women. There was a separate story about sins, and Melza realised she was a terrible sinner this time. The wretched girl must beg the Lord for forgiveness all her life because she was born in a cursed place and to cursed people. Only on the second cycle after that meeting did she decide that she had misinterpreted the words of the martyr since Morbus could not be mistaken.

This time, Morbus announced that they would beg for someone's toothache and stomach pain to go away, and for the return of a lost goat and a good tock harvest. Of course, they would all beg for the cursed townspeople's destruction and for the return of the villagers' primordial wealth. The martyr began with an old legend about two brothers who argued over who owned a cow. A passing sage suggested that they resolve the dispute very simply: to whoever's yard the cow will come, there it shall stay. He took the cow to pasture, and the brothers began to arrange their yards so that the cow would prefer it. Melza didn't listen to the end of the story but slowly moved away to the wicker fence and disappeared into the high bean thickets.

She had her own goal. For several cycles, curiosity had wrestled with fear and finally won. She had to get to Morbus's house and see what was written on those vablish leaves scattered on the floor of the room behind the bedroom. This was the only room she was not allowed to clean, and the secret to her strange experience a few cycles ago must be hidden there.

A guard with a spear outside the house was still awake. All the villagers had similar weapons – a long pole with one sharpened end, and some sharp stones, bones, iron and unusually sharp salt shards tied to the other end with wire, a chain, or welded together by a travelling blacksmith. Melza stood behind the tree for almost a thousand heartbeats before the guard stopped watching the chickens roaming nearby; he hung on his spear by force of habit, its heavy end standing on the ground. As always, at the sight of chickens, Melza experienced a painful nostalgia for the farm, where there were many animals, including chickens, caperturkeys, ostriches and thickneckers.

The guard had slept on duty many times before and soon started to snore. But he could easily wake up at the slightest rustle. So Melza silently tiptoed around him and entered the empty house. During begging, it was always empty here. The girl immediately went to the bedroom and lifted the hide, behind which a mysterious room was hidden.

The room wasn't big. It had a small ventilation hole in the east wall instead of a window. In addition to an unusually high table, it had baskets of various sizes on it, and between two sticks, a whitish skin with a scribbled map of the nearest town was stretched out. Melza recognised it, as she had seen it many times at the tram stops. The skin looked suspiciously human, but it was a blobster's skin bought by a merchant in another village.

The black sheets of vablish leaves weren't on the floor any more but were very neatly stacked on the table. Melza took one in her hands. It was dry but quite elastic. Had they been soaked in some oil? The room wasn't dark enough for the glowing dye to show on the surface of the leaves. The meagre but still sufficient light from the red dwarf came through an air hole. Melza tried to block the tiny window with one hand, but the light still leaked through her thin fingers. She lifted the lid off one of the baskets and used it as a shield. There were some translucent blue rocks in the basket, but she hardly acknowledged them. In the thicker darkness, the inscriptions lit up on the black sheets. There were strange symbols and numbers, but Melza understood only two words: "jamming" and "diapason."

From outside, a distant howl sounded. So the begging songs had started. Melza sighed.

Someone coughed loudly as if from under the table, but no one was there. Melza shuddered and dropped the leaf and the basket lid. Her stomach felt doused with ice water, and her heart pounded, almost in her throat. She tried to be quiet, but someone obviously had enhanced ears.

"Who is there?" she heard a weak and hoarse voice say. It actually came from under the floor.

Melza lay down on the three-layer rug and put her ear to it. Someone was breathing hoarsely just half a metre below her. So she was right. There was a room under the floor. A burial, probably.

Melza wanted to ask the standard question, "Is anyone there?" But she remembered her decision to remain loyal to O'Teka and didn't waste time on the obvious.

"Are you a prisoner?" she asked instead.

A muffled male voice answered, "Yes? Are you here alone?"

Melza felt terrified that the prisoner might betray her for a favour from the martyr.

"Yes. You're not from the village, are you?" she asked.

"No. I am from the main colony. My name is Davon Marchel. It feels like I've been here for over a month, but I am not sure any more."

Melza sighed with relief. "I am Melza. What can I do for you?"

"Quite a lot if you are so kind." Davon went quiet for a moment, "Listen, Melza. You sound like a child but not a local one."

"This is my second year here. I am sixteen."

"I see. Banished?"

"No. Just stupid. I ran away from home."

Davon didn't reply at first but then asked, "Do you want to get back?"

Melza had already answered this question to herself many times, so she said miserably, "Yes ... yes and yes."

The sound under the floor resembled a chuckle, but it was approving rather than mocking. "You have a chance to earn forgiveness. You are so young."

Melza felt excited for the first time in ages. "But how? I thought that is not possible. I will do my best if it is."

"Okay. Then get me a blade. Anything sharp. Even if it's bone. Then leave this place. Understand? Run from here to the south-west border and go along it to the western gate. Stay there until the patrol calls out to you. Tell them about me."

"They won't believe my words. I am a villager."

"They will believe you if you say you must talk to a brown orderman about the fire in the capital. That fire happened because of me."

Melza grabbed the edge of the rug and lifted it up. Between the clay slabs was a gap through which you could place your fingers but not your whole hand. Melza looked into it and saw two silver pupils quite close together.

"Because of you?"

"Yes."

"But how?"

"I will tell them myself. They will know how to get me out. The colony is in danger. The temple is in trouble. Will you do this? Don't worry. You won't be forced to come back after such news. It is too serious."

"I understood everything. Wait a minute."

The girl got up and listened to what was going on outside the house walls. At least three begging songs remained before the service would end.

Melza looked around the secret room but didn't find any sharp objects. In the martyr's bedroom, her eyes fell on that horrifying basket covered with a dark cloth by the bed. Well, of course. She had always been afraid to touch it because she knew what was in it. But now, although she was even more frightened than usual, she knelt beside it and carefully lifted the cloth with two fingers. Those dark splodges on it were definitely blood. And at the bottom of the basket was a kitchen knife, a medical scalpel and half a pair of scissors. The scalpel looked sharp and thin enough to Melza. She grabbed it, hurried back, and lowered it into the gap between the floor tiles.

"Oh, okay! Thanks, this will do nicely. What won't you find now in the villages of the wild lands?" Davon laughed again. "Now, Melza, you need to take care of yourself. Go. Go now. If the villagers catch you, tell the martyr you have no memories of doing any of it. Morbus will believe you, don't you worry."

Melza put the rug back in place, cleaned up the traces of her stay, and slowly approached the door.

The guard was still dozing while standing, hanging on his spear, and he didn't see Melza tiptoe past him and run home. For the first time, she was glad that her "hemisphere" was not guarded. She grabbed an empty pear flask for water, her old backpack, a knitted coat and a piece of goatskin shaped like a bonnet. In case of rain, she could cover her head and neck with it, or use it as a pouch.

She was already on her way to the creek when she heard a distant thump on the signal drum membrane. The service had ended.

Melza missed that cycle's food distribution, but her absence wasn't noticed until the next cycle, when the goat shepherds discovered that she hadn't collected and washed the soup bowls for them.

13. In the Temple

Cesario, unlike Viola, had a physical body capable of moving inside the temple of O'Teka. It was a humanoid biological body, quite tall and muscular. He required electrical and chemical nourishment, air and some form of rest. His central nervous system was limited by the hindbrain's organic tissue and a whole, although wired, spinal cord. His skull was mainly filled with a remarkable piece of neuroware. And his body was adapted to it pretty much in the loader's way. But if the loader was a human with added computer elements, Cesario was AI with a body. Like Vist, he dressed in a hooded robe, but no one doubted that Cesario was a man. His voice was human, not very low, but male. His face was covered with a black velvet mask with not a single hole in it. But that mask was mostly hidden behind the holographic face, which was different every cycle. Cesario was unable to come up with a unique face, so he chose someone else's for himself, favouring his heroes. That cycle he wore the face of Alan Turing.

Cesario's sister Viola, also created by the architexter, was restricted to Vist's mansion and was nothing but a program within the premises, with a female voice and always the same face on the holoscreens. The face looked a lot like Vist's but younger.

Both Viola and Cesario worked well together and were mostly controlled by Vist. They were Vist's extensions, assistants, caretakers, overseers and ... only O'Teka knows what else.

Vist and his assistant greeted each other in passing, and the backs of their hands barely touched. In that fraction of a second, Vist felt a slight uneasiness in Cesario's artificial rib and in one of the vertebrae and received a report invisible to anyone else.

"Master Vist, an anonymous attempt was made at the temple to gain access to your personal data. It was detected eight minutes and forty-seven seconds ago and lasted for one minute and nine seconds. I can confirm fourteen workers and visitors were in the temple then. Timofey has gathered them all in one of the conference rooms."

"Thank you," Vist said aloud.

"Can I assist you at all? Master Architexter?" Cesario also asked in his soft voice.

"Yes, please. Master McLeod will be here in a few minutes. He will bring one of the scout tools. Could you please adapt it to use in the dwelling areas and make a few working copies? I will tell Mr Hesley to temporarily turn off the auto-cleaners."

"Very well. I will do my best."

One hour later, Cesario and Steven entered the conference room together, carrying a handful of what looked like intricate small goblets. Now Cesario's face resembled James Watt's from the local school portrait. They found Vist with a group of people at the oval table having a lunch served by Timofey.

Steven said, "Andrea asked me to mention that the scouting agency wrote off the old weather-band model and sold them all to farmers. A dead end. Sorry, Vist. What's going on here?"

Vist got up and walked Steven and Cesario back to the corridor for a private update.

There weren't any suspicious strangers among those present at the temple. Even among the visitors, two guests from the southern fish farm were found walking the museum and hadn't been near the terminals. All the employees were trusted people, and the amulets of students and one historian showed exactly which archives they were connected to during the breach.

"So? How does this thing work?" asked Vist, taking one of the goblets and studying it.

"You connect it like this to the amulet and turn it on." Cesario gave a demonstration, synchronising one of the goblets to Steven's chest badge. "The device interferes with the natural diffusion of particles in the air. Therefore, I shaped it to collect samples in small regions such as rooms, corridors or doorways. It can even work on the street if you hold it close to the ground. The funnel part starts to take the air in slowly, as if inhaling. You can read the detected particles on the screen or vocalise them in your earpiece."

Timofey watched them closely. This small round man with very dark-purple pigmented skin laughed and said, "Master, you want to try and use the ancient method and find the problem by its smell. With no trained dog at hand, you have a chemical detector."

"Yes, Mr Hesley. I was going to use it elsewhere, but this will be a good test. Take one each and check our suspects. Cesario will check the scholars. Steven, the city visitors are yours. Timofey and I will 'sniff' the staff members."

For many future generations of scientists and scouts, ordermen and the Law Force, the chemical detector modified by Cesario would be called a "sniffer." This device was used in a criminal investigation for the first time during that cycle. It found one compound that should not be in the temple archives. Phlogopite mica molecules were found in the hands of Elya Goryn.

Vist sent Steven with new detectors to Mik and his squad. He ordered Timofey to let the others go, took Elya into the next room, and silently studied the frightened face of the young man. Elya turned pale and, unable to bear the architexter's look, sat down on the floor and covered his eyes with his hands. He was evidently waiting for questions, but Vist remained still. This guy is a colonist. He must know what is expected of him.

And indeed, Elya gathered his courage, got back on his feet and spoke, although he still avoided Vist's eye. "I was running an errand for which I was promised that Phoebe would be returned to me intact. She didn't answer my calls all cycle, but Groonya did. She said that Phoebe wanted to go to the temple, and I had to find her if she wasn't there. Otherwise, Mr Baker would worry himself to the grave. I ran home to get my conbike, and there was an inscription on the wall that read, 'Deliver the envelope to the temple, don't tell anyone, and Phoebe won't be hurt.' And there was also an instruction to erase the message so that no traces were left. I cleaned the wall, but before doing so, I took an image of it with my amulet."

"Wise," Vist said and lifted their fingers towards the boy's shoulder. "May I see it?"

"Of course, sir ... ma'am!"

The architexter touched Elya's epaulette for no more than two seconds and said, "Go on."

Elya breathed out and carried on, "The envelope lay right there on the floor. I opened it. It wasn't a bomb." Elya finally looked directly into Vist's face. "Believe me, sir! I am a mechanic, but—"

"I know," Vist said softly.

Elya wiped his wet forehead with his sleeve and continued his story. "It was a typical greetings holo-card with a musical hologram included inside. At least the mechanism was very similar. If it wasn't for Phoebe having gone missing, I would have thought someone was trying to deliver a surprise gift. So I brought the envelope to the temple and was going to take it straight to Mr Hesley as soon as Phoebe's amulet responded to my call. The instructions didn't say what to do next. I was so worried."

Elya stopped talking and his face looked puzzled.

"Well?" said Vist.

"Ma'am … I'm not sure what happened next. I went towards my workshop and … I remember … I was holding the envelope in my left hand. And the next thing – I was falling off the lowest step of the maintenance stairs that lead from the essays archive to the weather monitoring room. I was lucky to grab the railing, otherwise, I would have broken my neck."

Elya lifted the sleeve of his work gown and showed his elbow to the architexter. The arm above his left elbow was swollen, a few scales were torn off, and drops of fresh blood shone like scarlet beads.

"Did this happen during the fall?"

"No, ma'am. Apparently, I had already fallen before, but I have no memory of that. Where that envelope went, I can't tell."

Vist closed his eyes and called, "Cesario?"

"I'm almost there," Cesario replied. "It's just a few steps from the compromised terminal. The boy is telling the truth. The auto-cleaner hasn't washed away his blood in the archive yet."

Vist opened their eyes and asked Elya, "Why didn't you tell me about it during lunch?"

"I couldn't think straight, Sir. I thought I was going crazy and didn't immediately connect my blackout with the violation. Also, Phoebe never answered. That was all I could think of."

This time, Vist touched their own amulet above the left ear, and Elya heard the dear voice in less than a minute.

"Hello? Master Architexter, what can I do you for?"

"Its okay, Miss Baker. One of my employees is concerned about your well-being."

"Elya? I sincerely apologise that he took your time. I'm fine. We just got back from the seashore. There was no signal."

"Thank you, Phoebe. Vist out."

The call ended before Elya asked, "We?"

"Mr Goryn, I have the means to find out who she was with. Our satellite can answer that question, and I advise you not to compromise the investigation further by questioning Phoebe yourself."

"Understood, sir. I failed you and my purpose. I am prepared for any consequences."

"You had no bad intentions, and your only crime was to allow your fear to cloud your reason. No harm has been done yet as far as I can tell. Go now."

As soon as Elya left the room, Vist heard Cesario's voice.

"Master, I found an envelope with the device inside. It looks like a holo-message, but I think it is something else. How shall I proceed? Give it to Timofey for analysis?"

"No, work with it yourself and away from our guests and employees. At least at the same distance Elya was from the envelope when he came to his senses."

14. Obydva

Obydva brought the wheelchair to the edge of a marble pool full of water lilies, partially shaded by a road bridge above it.

"Is this where it happened?" Rod asked, "Are you telling me that you remember?"

"No," Obydva replied, "I know what it is, but I don't have any memories of this place. I remember some feelings I had never experienced. Suffocation or drowning. Since my upload, I have not been keen on diving or swimming."

They were silent for a while, and then Rod asked again, "What other feelings do you remember? I mean, the ones you have no experience of?"

"Some tastes and smells. There is no vodka on Noverca, and I have never drunk it before, but I know its taste and effect. I miss Phoebe and Groonya. I missed you."

"But Marta adored my girls too. And they missed Marta. I know they were off to Carib in turns to see you more than once. Plus, she and I were friends for a long time."

"You might be right. I miss Martin and Chang too."

Rod changed the subject. "Have you heard that Mr Larsson remarried? Now what is her name? Mmm ... Hesley's widow?"

"Yes. And I am happy for both of them." Obydva turned Rod's chair around to face him. "I need to ask you something important. Why did you give up? You are heading for the end. You don't even write any more. Why don't you let Vist upload you too? This is so cruel to us all."

Almost disappeared in wrinkles, Rod's eyes were wet. He tried to turn his head away, but it is not easy when you can hardly move. "I am no use to anyone here. I can do nothing."

"You are a burden to the girls, you old stump!" Obydva said the words but didn't sound angry. "Groonya should be working on her future with Jaxon, dating like crazy, making career and family plans. She has no life at all, as she is spending her youth looking after Phoebe and becoming your nurse. Phoebe, too, will not leave Groonya to look after you alone, and she refuses to see that boy."

"You can't tell me what to do. It was up to me to grow old and die. I don't know why it's taking so long."

"You made a similar decision for me a generation ago, didn't you?" Obydva sat on the bench and took Rod's hand between his large palms. "Steven told me. He was right next to you on that day."

"Ha! Never thought you would become a cook though!"

"And here we are!"

"But I am useless. I didn't want to run the farm without you and sold it to Jaxon."

"But you still finished the book. It is taught in schools now."

"It saved me from grief. When I mourned you. But I couldn't build things here because I am nothing but an antiquity in the engineering world."

"You could write books and invent things again – new things. Back on Earth, every time the famous Rod Baker developed a new fantastic machine ... what did he say?" Obydva coughed and imitated a cockney with an Asian accent, "This was a lemon squeezie! Just a prototype for my next masterpiece. I was just practising."

He smiled, and Rod couldn't stop himself chuckling gloomily, but he stopped almost immediately. "Hey, you're not supposed to remember that?"

Obydva let his hand go and said very quietly. "I am not supposed to love you either," and then added more loudly, "Oh, look. It's Vist and Nat. Right on time. I invited Vist to meet us here for a chat."

After all the greetings, Vist asked, "Where are your daughters, Rod?"

"I'm not sure," Rod replied. "I think Groonya went to look for Phoebe. She could be out on a date."

"Why don't we check this out," Nat said, "Let me take you home?"

Obydva agreed to cook dinner later at Rod's house, and then Rod and Nat left the park. The two loaders sat beside each other on a bench by the pool. Their hands rested on the seat, with the back of Vist's fingers barely touching the knuckles of Obydva's left hand. From the side, it looked like two people were enjoying a moment of peace while listening to the waterfall. But they were having a very important conversation. While they could communicate through touch, they still felt impolite doing so with friends around. Even among other loaders.

Obydva asked, "I can feel something is wrong. What are you up to? Do I need to worry about the girls?"

"No more than usual, as far as I can tell presently. We just had a word with Elya Goryn."

"The young man we met yesterday? Why?"

"A few hours ago, he couldn't get Phoebe to answer the call. Then he found this note on the wall of his house. Look."

Both loaders closed their eyes for a second at the same time.

Obydva turned to look at Vist, "That resembles the graffiti on the burned factory you showed me earlier. The same author?"

"Or his messenger."

"Was Phoebe really kidnapped?"

"No, she just went for a walk outside the city walls with a friend. Her signal there was blocked by regular radiation. But the boy believed the threat and agreed to break the rules to rescue the love of his life. He went to the temple area, which he had access to as a mechanic. All he had to do was deliver this envelope to the spire and keep quiet about it."

Obydva rolled his left eye.

"A holo-card? Was it for you? It looks festive and tastefully made."

"A card with a very interesting piece of technology inside. Note, please, that the front and back are decorated with a wafer-thin, translucent turquoise mineral. No, the card is not a bomb, but I have an idea about its function. Cesario is working on it now, but it was active for less than two minutes and then went dead. I think it was just tested, but we are not sure yet what for and whether it passed the sender's test."

"So what about the boy? Did Mik arrest him?"

"No need. Steve and Mik are roaming the city with detectors looking for phlogopite mica, traces of which I found on Elya and his envelope. Blue salt includes a high percentage of mica, which links this card with that blue totem from the assassin's memory. There isn't much mica in the town – just the sand in the city garden and this pond. But outside the city walls, there is more of it, if not in a concentrated form. The last I heard from Steven was that the 'sniffer' led him to the southern borders of the colony."

"To the port?"

"Yes. Obydva, it is time we talk about you. You said it was important."

"I'm not sure any more. You and the guys have enough on your plate to worry about without my little problem."

"Let me decide. You would not come all this way. I know it wasn't just for a funeral." Vist smiled and said aloud, "Tell me, don't make me scan you."

Obydva cleared his throat. "All right. I never could say no to you. As you know, one of my most popular menus includes vareniki with spiced *nix fossores.* Or, as the nordians called them, snowpillars."

Vist nodded. "Those finger-like white creatures that feed on the snow algae? Tasty indeed. No wonder they're popular."

"As you can't farm nix in the hot Pettogreko islands, I arranged a deal with researchers working at a seismic station in the permafrost. Their automatic plane, which they call the cargo-avion, comes in from the north once a month and brings me a few kilograms of living nix, and they aren't cheap, I can tell you that." Obydva sniffed and continued. "Now it is few cycles late, but my attempts to contact the station have failed. They do not answer, and I doubt this is a picnic out of town with the whole company. In the colony, only you and Timofey have access to the cameras on the satellite. I decided to talk to you before disturbing Grand."

"I see. Did you know them well? Did they chat about their work there?"

Obydva shrugged. "I don't know them at all, as I went there only once to see the owner and set the terms. The monthly cargo-avion is automatic, and is received and reprogrammed in Carib by the assisting service. The station hasn't used a human pilot for years. I know that there are about twenty station dwellers, and they catch the nix easily, luring them into traps with a vibrating instrument that measures the thickness of the ice. They cook nix too – in soup."

"They have dangerous neighbours there who also feed on snowpillars," Vist added.

"I asked once if they were afraid of the svoloch, but they laughed and said that the svoloch were wise enough not to come close to the station, and that they had not seen one for five or six years."

"Sure, Nat will be happy to fly there and have a look. He has his own search team now."

"Vist, I still worry about Nat every time he goes off on a dangerous mission."

"But he loves it. If it makes you feel better, I will go with him."

Obydva squinted at Vist and laughed. "You love it too! I know you well enough now. You would not miss an opportunity. You grow so bored in your spire with no breaking news."

"Would you pilot *Wasp* for me?" Vist asked.

Obydva stopped laughing, "No. My piloting days are over."

"You still come here on your old hideous avion."

"It is the fastest transport I have, but I plan to use it in emergencies only."

Vist covered Obydva's hand with his and gently squeezed. "Oh, I didn't realise," he said. "How far?"

"Fourteen weeks."

"Did you bank or use an egg donor?"

"There's not much left in the Earth gene bank, but I found what I wanted."

"Marta's?"

"Yes. It is already in the artificial womb, but please do not share the news just yet."

"This is amazing news! Congratulations. Where is it?"

"In Carib. I want to return there as soon as possible."

"Well, no need to waste any time. Just let me get some updates from the guys, and if everything is going well ..." Vist hesitated. "Are you going to tell Rod?"

"Still thinking about it."

Vist nodded and closed his eyes to contact Mik. General King responded immediately.

"Cesario has some advice for you on the blue salt. Did you hear from him?" Vist asked.

"Yes, he suggests checking the art workshops."

"That's right. Did you instruct your men?"

"Right away. They reported that one of the sculptors fulfilled the anonymous client's request for a chemical casting. Nothing complicated – but his description fits our geometric totem made of blue salt. And the inside frame was already provided – wires, some metal scrap. He thought nothing of it, but are you thinking what I am thinking? Vist? Do you remember when Nat found a ship full of svoloch in the northern ice? Noah-4? It remained invisible even to the satellite because of the blue salt all around it? Vist?"

Obydva saw Vist turning pale, probably for the first time ever. Vist said slowly and quietly, "Mica is an electrical insulator, but blue salt has other properties. That thing wasn't a totem. It was an undetectable device that would not arouse suspicion in or out of the city."

15. Danielle

Steven took a deep breath of sea air and exhaled noisily, admiring the stunning view of the horizon.

Mik got off the driver's seat but didn't join him, still looking back. Steven shaded his eyes with his hand and peered into the ocean waters. It was quite light here, almost cloudless, and Vitr stood still a little higher and peered out from behind the southern dunes.

"Mik, you sit in your office and don't know how many changes are happening daily. Stop glaring at the road. Danielle will arrive here from a different direction."

Mik turned his head. "There's only one way out of the town."

"If we needed to meet someone from the town, we would go to one of the restaurants in Altyn District. Mik, you told me to find a specialist on the south-eastern coast of Gera because the mica trail brought us here. Dani knows the geography of those places best of all and swims faster than other cadets."

"Have you started accepting ikhtees into the academy?"

"Five years ago. Did you miss that? Oh, man, they are so ready! A whole age group under twenty-five does not have to submit to monthly medical check-ups or even leave the depths of Lantida if not necessary for business or service."

"And how many do you have in your academy?"

"So far, only forty new recruits and sixteen graduates."

Mik didn't have time to say anything in response. One of the lazy long green waves slithering towards the grey beach was bulging. They saw a vertebral fin, and a second later, the head and shoulders of Agent Danielle Mirovska rose out of the water. It was quite an eye-feast.

The water was not deep, and she had to walk about twenty paces before her voice could be heard. The agent wore a tight ucha wetsuit that hugged her body from the shoulder straps to her knees. Vitr's reddish light reflected brilliantly off the wet fabric and the pale dolphin skin. Agent Mirovska's head was smooth and shiny, and her eyes were small and devoid of eyelashes. Ikhtees don't have mermaid hair as this would only make them less streamlined. Instead, a membranous ridge stretched from her nose bridge, over her head, and then all the way to her lower back. Its scientific name was *combfin*, but even if he had known this word once, Steven could not remember it now. The blond philanderer simply enjoyed the sight of the marine inhabitant's elongated and flexible forms, but Mik didn't look impressed.

"Master McLeod! No calm, no storm to you!" a pleasant soprano voice said to Steven.

"No ice, no steam!" he replied joyfully.

As the academy graduate emerged from the water and climbed the pier boards, Steven hinted that Mik should have watched artificial mutation for the past forty years. But when he introduced Mik to the young agent, he couldn't tell whether his friend shared his like for this smooth and wet face with a dark-grey nose bridge and scaly specks on the cheekbones and neck.

"Report, Danielle," Steven ordered, looking at Mik and thinking as usual, Ah, if only we were seventy years younger.

"Over the past five weeks, the number of active fishing sailboats on the islands has not changed. I checked the readings from Japheth, the submarine operating in these waters. It showed a boat that had never recorded a voyage from the mainland to the island of Pettogreco. The vessel was scanned at the port, but nothing suspicious was found. The purpose of the trip was reefscape sketching and private watercolour lessons. It's a long but safe route for a small boat to follow the chain of reefs."

"And that's all?" Steven asked, deliberately stern.

"Yes, master. Your instructions were about suspicious ships and courses. Should I upload my report to the temple?"

"Yes. Just in case. Anything else to report? Anything that isn't usually entered into the official records?"

"Yes, sir. That's why I called you here. We are close to the ninth group of minor riffs. Do you see that small flat island? It is called Croc's Lip. Behind it, some tall rocks wriggle out of the water. We call

them Croc's Teeth." The girl turned and pointed
north with her webbed finger. "I often patrolled
these waters on the angler's request."

"Well?"

"I saw the dinghy with those people who said
they were artists. They didn't head to Pettogreco.
They arrived ashore on Croc's Lip but didn't sketch
anything."

"What were they doing then?" Steven
frowned.

"Nothing. They sat on the shore, empty-
handed and ... crooning.

"What? They were doing what?" Mik and
Steven asked at the same time.

"They mooed ... as if they were humming a
song. Only there was no melody."

"How many people were in there?" Mik
asked.

"Just two women. Looking pretty harmless."

Steven stopped staring at Danielle's arms
and made a note in the amulet on his badge. "So
listen, Dani, forget the fishing report. Everything
about that dinghy – from official to personal

observations – send directly to my mail. Who else can describe them?"

"The cadets Akemi and Sura may have seen them. Their plankton detour was only an hour after mine."

"Tell them to message me too. I want everything from all of you: a description of those two on board, their time of arrival and return, any activity your friends observed."

"Yes, sir."

Steven glanced at Mik and added, "And what did they have with them?"

"Nothing, sir. I didn't see any easels or laser brushes. Just something like a small statue. The size of a two-year-old codfish."

Mik asked with a stone face, "Is the codfish the size of a brandy bottle? What was it made of?" Danielle frowned as she remembered, and Mik said, "Looks like a piece of mineral. Like salt, only blue?"

Danielle's eyes widened almost to their normal size.

"Yes, sir. A tower of geometric shapes. The audit report does not mention this at all. How did you know?"

But Mik turned and walked quickly to the conmot parked by the road. Steven gave new instructions, reluctantly dismissed Danielle back into the sea, and hurried after Mik.

16. In the Mansion

On the second floor of the architexter's house, the middle of a wide living room was covered in packages of the latest upgraded equipment. Most were standard shoes, clothing and helmets for field scouts, mineralogists, biologists and pioneer novercologists. After all, the Gera continent had not yet been fully explored, mapped and described. The nearby islands, stretching west and east along the comfort zone, had recently become a popular terrain for amateur expeditions and business planners. The hardware institute had many contracts and orders and was doing very well, but Andrea Alloway took the time to put together a collection of novelties for the new Law Force.

Snacks and huge jars of kefir stood on the tables between the sofas. Uzhan's string music and birds chirping were barely audible from above. Nat and Steve looked at each item, comparing them to old equipment used in the early years of rescue trips. Mik didn't take part. He watched Vist in silence, frowning.

Vist was busy, sitting still with their eyes half-closed and irises narrowed. But the loader heard and saw everything that happened in the room, as if they were openly observing how Andrea thrust a pair of new boots into Nat's hands.

"Nat! Will you listen to me or not? When sliding, they will create the degree of friction you need. Like brakes in a conmot – you adjust it yourself. So don't worry, you won't slip, but they will be better than any skis for you in case they are needed. You told me you were better at skiing after your foot replacement."

"Snowboarding, darling."

"Same difference."

Nat turned to Mik and Steven with a sigh. "I envy you guys for staying single."

Andrea snorted and unwrapped the next thing she had brought.

"And we envy you that you married such a genius as Andrea," Steven said, rummaging through the pile of white gear. "Look at this jacket. Even scouts don't have such advanced luxury. It can be turned into a tent. You can't cut it with a knife, never mind with the teeth of a svoloch. Pants with a thermostat? Seriously? Nordians are daft to refuse good equipment. And what's that, Frau Alloway? Is that an artificial tentacle?"

"Yes, it's a synthetic third limb. When moving quickly, it allows you to keep your hands free if you are falling or if an obstacle arises. Good for climbing too."

"Brilliant! Vist, can I go instead of you? You have an investigation to run here."

Only Vist's lips moved when she or he answered, "Mik can handle it for a while. He needs your help on the riffs. Just stay in touch with Timofey if you need anything."

Andrea waved her hand in no particular direction, "I have new equipment for you and Mik too. Very similar, and the temperature is regulated in both directions, even if you go further south."

"But there is no snow."

"The camouflage is also adjustable. That is why I named this fabric 'chameleon.'"

"Yuck! So cheesy!" Nat laughed.

"Zina's idea, not mine. She said I needed a tacky but lovely name. It will sell better."

Mik was watching Vist from his corner and asked as soon as the architexter opened both eyes and looked at him.

"Well?"

"The answer might not be that far off. Obydva wants to know if the problem is intentional sabotage or a technical glitch. His suppliers of the northern delicacy sent his goods from the permafrost by the fairly regular cargo craft. This time the computer-controlled avion fell before reaching the warm zone. I checked the crash site on a satellite camera and spotted an object in the snow nearby. It has a humanoid shape, and it is still there."

"So there was a pilot this time?" Mik frowned.

"Who might be dead. But the avion computer should be fine, so it might tell me what I need to know. We are taking *Wasp* and will be back before you find the totem. Please ask Zina to be prepared to receive the patient, just in case the pilot is still alive, or something is wrong at the station."

"No problem. How many people are you taking with you?"

"Just Nat. Obydva said there could be about twenty scientists. *Wasp* can take that many of the nordians' size, but only just."

"Just make sure you call for help if needed. We don't have a spaceship, but Steve and I can still be with you in a cycle or so in Obydva's Bumblebag!"

"I am sure he will keep it ready." Vist turned and looked Mik in the eyes, "Mik, what do your instincts tell you so far? Is there any connection?"

Mik shrugged. "North is where our blue salts came from. Also timing. Nothing happened in decades, and suddenly so many events have occurred within a week."

Nat's happy laughter interrupted them. He was wearing a newly modified helmet with protective visors.

"It's like a loader's full upgrade! I can hear the heartbeats not only of all five of us but also of another two approaching. They are at the gate. I am loving it."

"It must be Zina and Scarlett. We are having dinner at Rod's," said Andrea.

"Again? Fantastic!" Steven said, "Let's go down and meet them in the hall. Hey, Mik, Rod's girl ... Groonya ... has grown up to be a real beauty."

"Don't even think about her, old sport," Nat said, "Obydva is still strong enough to rip your head off."

"I am joking. Calm down. I invited Danielle to be my date."

"Your former cadet? She is an ikhtees and also too young for you. To her, you will be like water off a duck's back," said Andrea. "Now, Mik, please help me to take all these downstairs."

"Vist, catch up," Steven called from the door.

Soon their voices and laughter died out in the distance. All but the architexter left the house to meet with Mrs Darkwood and Da Costa's widow.

Vist sat still for a while and then said, "Viola, call out for the satellite again. Enter the station coordinates and look for any signs of activity around the station."

Vist closed their eyes again and said without making a sound, "Camera, 8 degrees west ... move 150 metres ... stop. Magnify. Now 60 metres to the right ... Hmmm. Follow that ridge ... another 1,000 metres. Again, stop. What is that?"

"Are you asking me, master?" Viola replied. "How would I know?"

"Remind you of anything?"

"Animal footprints. Species ... unknown. Not likely a quadrupedal animal, though. Is this a problem?"

"The prints themselves? No. The problem is – yes, scale it – that they are huge. Their average is no less than eight square metres."

"Average?"

"Yes. Look closely. The size and shape are inconsistent. Magnify a little more. Thank you. Those large prints are surrounded by numerous human footprints. Hmm, I think Nat and I will have to skip that dinner."

17. Blue Salt

Karlina hated communication rituals so much she could hardly contain herself. But it was too late to back out. She understood that she had not only become bogged down in this heinous intrigue but had also drawn her daughter in. So much so that she wouldn't get off with rehabilitation for the both of them. Matilda sat in the chair in front of her with closed eyes, and swayed from side to side. Between them on the table stood the new decognitivator, which was like a styled tower model or stained stalagmite. The shadow of the blue salt's translucent figure was also bluish, and the indicator's tiny light glowed in the crystal's depths. As always, both women experienced a terrible headache during the ritual, but the stronger and more experienced Karlina didn't let someone else's will into her mind

VIST & PROPER GANDA

as easily as poor Tilda did.

At last, the tiny light died out, and her daughter stopped humming and swaying and opened her eyes. The farmer already knew this look, but she still asked carefully, "Morbus? Is that you?"

The strange grin on Tilda's face was the answer. "It's nice and cool here. Tea and fruits? I am thankful. But you overestimate my overtake degree. I can't fully appreciate the taste or smell yet."

Karlina almost got up to take away the tray full of snacks and slices of sea melon but didn't want to appear too cordial. "When you first connected, you felt nothing at all. Do you have access to more of the central nervous system?"

"I like this model better," said a calm and confident voice, but the words didn't address Karlina. "Well done, Davon. This time the connection is faster and less dazzling. But there is still much resistance in the city, I can feel it." Morbus finally lifted her eyes to Karlina. "You must tell Matilda to find out from her former lover if Melza, the daughter of a poultry keeper, who has run away from me, has appeared here. My people are looking for her in other villages, but she could have made her way into the city, although this is unlikely."

Morbus's right hand went up to scratch her forearm, but this time Matilda was dressed in the scout's dense jacket of ucha-silk. Karlina ordered it in advance and paid a lot of money for it. She suppressed a light desire to gloat and asked, "How many models has Davon already assembled for you?"

Morbus spoke slowly, without looking at Karlina. She seemed to be thinking out loud. "It doesn't matter. What's important is that only a miserable five per cent are still amenable to influence in the colony. Most susceptible citizens are children under ten or hysterical failures like your daughter. And, ironically, they are not the type of people who have access to useful archives. Villagers are much easier, and svolochs are the easiest. They are all as simple as kids, so it's the other way around with them. You should have seen, Karlina, what they can do for me under especially intense stress. I can wind them up and synchronise their primitive heads in such a way that I control hundreds as one. If there were twenty times more of them, they would erase the colony's borders for me."

"Then what good are savages to you?"

Morbus slowly looked towards the window and around the room. "Not much yet, but they have great potential. They might become an army mostly incapable of thinking for themselves. They would complete unpaid and hardy labour and, having lost their sense of self-preservation, would do anything for me. I can inspire them with any absurdity without even threatening them too much. The svolochs collected a lot of material for devices at the station and a lot of blue salt for my work. They successfully sabotaged the nordians' transport and communications, but one resistant individual attempted to break the decognitivator and, therefore, their common obedience to me. I saw it through the eyes of one of the savages and ordered them to kill the saboteur. Hopefully, the rest learned their lesson."

"And your experiment with that boy? How did it go?"

"He is smart, and I was able to master his will for less than five minutes. He went where I ordered him to go, but his resistance was so great that I didn't have time to see anything in the temple's archives."

"He wouldn't have done even this if he hadn't been worried about his woman."

Morbus fell into deep thought and stared at the decognitivator once again. Karlina waited, watching the Great Martyr absentmindedly run her fingers along the tight sleeve.

"Karlina, you have just confirmed my greatest theory," said Morbus at last, still without looking up. Dim eyes continued to stare into the dark-blue crystal on the table, "We need to conduct a new experiment. The townspeople have a strong will and intellect, but if they are taken when out of emotional balance, they may be more accommodating, just like that moaning short person. It wasn't an accident after all."

"And how are you going to experiment?" Karlina asked, raising her eyebrows.

Morbus didn't answer but slowly turned her gaze to Karlina. In the next second, the Great Martyr grabbed a fruit knife from the tray, raised it to Matilda's face, and cut her right cheek from the corner of her lip to her ear.

Matilda couldn't fully feel the pain, but her face contorted, and a groan broke through the will of Morbus. Karlina screamed and rushed to her daughter to grab her hands, but she froze, gritting her teeth with rage.

However, Morbus was also in pain, which she didn't expect. The Great Martyr held the will of both women for no more than two seconds and soon left Matilda's consciousness. Once free, Matilda burst into tears, grabbed a tea towel from the tray, and pressed it to her face. The cut on her cheek was deep, and the towel was immediately soaked with blood.

"Mama!" she whimpered, bending forwards and trembling. She didn't know what to do, as one look at her mother told her this wasn't Karlina any more.

"That's better. Now you can tell me everything yourself. Don't worry. Karlina knows she shouldn't resist so as not to waste time. The sooner we're done, the sooner she can stitch you up."

It was difficult for Matilda to speak. Extremely salty Novercian tears flooded her face and seeped into the wound, intensifying the pain. "I have nothing to tell you. You already know I'm only allowed in the entertainment department and on the temple's study floors. They don't take me to the conference room where the architexter and the investigation team arrange their meetings. Steven is avoiding me because of your antics. Doctor Darkwood despises me. Phoebe doesn't know anything, and Scarlett won't go to the mansion after your first time with her."

"But you have been there, too."

"That was before you used my hands to set fire to the factory."

"But did you see anything in the museum or the house? Any mummy or tomb, canned organisms or TPS tanks?"

"No. The loader kept such things in the laboratory, and no one can get there except for other loaders."

With a roar, Morbus swept the tray of fruit and cups off the table with both hands. "So you are of no use to me! Even talking to you is boring. Be grateful I still need your mother. Otherwise—"

Morbus suddenly fell silent and stared at her right hand, or rather at Karlina's hand. She pondered it, reached up to the table's smooth surface and ran her fingers over it. Then she raised those same fingers to her eyes, rubbed the fingers together, and grinned. Her hand slowly went for the hem of Matilda's striped dress, but then Karlina made an effort herself, and Morbus left them be.

Karlina rushed to her daughter and wrapped her arms around her.

"I am so sorry! My baby! I shouldn't have let this happen. I shouldn't have let this svoloch use us like this."

"Ma, I can't take it any more!" Matilda sobbed.

"We need to take care of this cut first. The clinic is not far. Come on."

Matilda rose to her feet with a groan. She swayed. "Please, mum! Let's stop all this. I'll tell Steven."

Karlina dragged her daughter by the hand to the garage, to her farm truck. "No! Nothing good will come of this. We need those pears. Your father may be a fool, but he warned me: if I trade with the villages, then one cycle, instead of paying me, they will offer sheer blackmail and threats." She pushed her bleeding daughter into the truck and got behind the wheel. "Looks like, after all, I'm not much smarter than him."

On the way to the emergency room, Matilda's bleeding stopped, and her accelerated regeneration began – one of the first artificial adaptations for second-wave Earth evacuees and their children. She was checked for infection on arrival at the clinic, and the treatment was properly directed and controlled. But it took many hours before the wound healed completely, leaving behind a thin but noticeable scar.

18. Steven

Steven kept his gear in his workshop, which served as a garage whenever he could create a new working vehicle. This time, in the middle of a vast room, lay the frame of a rock climber, a very popular vehicle on Mars at the beginning of colonisation. He entered the house, then he stopped and stared in surprise at the electronic lock's blinking orange light, which indicated that someone uninvited was inside.

Steven had been locking the doors again since he and his comrades were kidnapped many years ago. And recent events forced him to take this signal very seriously. He froze, turning on all his abilities and experiences. He closed his eyes and listened, concentrating all his perceptions on identifying the intruder.

He heard one person in his house settled into one of the second floor rooms. He listened to that person pouring something into a glass and snacking on something crunchy, most likely ... well, of course. Peppery breadsticks with dried herbs and spices, which Steven had bought last week in New Tokyo. Music played in the uninvited guest's amulet.

From this music, Steven understood who had come to him. He sighed in annoyance, muttered, "You've got to be kidding me!" and went upstairs.

Matilda lay in a deep armchair, her head thrown back as she chewed on the snack. Her lilac throat was exposed and moved in waves. Her amulet, a huge pendant, rose and fell with every breath. And a furrow of silvery scales shimmered seductively, from cheekbones to bare collarbones. On the table nearby stood a glass of white wine that Mik had supplied to Steven's collection.

When Steven entered the room, she opened her eyes and turned her head without getting up.

"I've been waiting," she said with a smile.

"What are you doing here?" Steven asked, noticing that the woman was not dressed for a business visit.

"What do you think? I'm scared. The recent fire, the farewell ritual, and the anxiety in the town influenced me. You're all now busy looking for bad guys, but there were no assignments for poor Tilda. And inaction has such a depressing effect on me."

"Since when?" Steven asked and picked up an open bottle. Damn it. She opened the Caribs Estate Chardonnay, which he was saving for the New Year. "Why didn't you go to your mother's farm again?"

"Mother is not exactly fun company since my father has left. It escapes me why she didn't follow him."

"Because your father betrayed O'Teka, and your mother is a true follower."

"Anyway, I don't feel safe with her. I feel safe with you, Stefan." Matilda stood up and approached Steven. Her dress was the same dress she had on when Steven first saw her at the temple. It still fitted well but looked better on her in her late twenties than now. Steven noticed a fresh scar on Tilda's cheek, generously powdered with purple glitter. He would have asked what happened in normal circumstances, but now he didn't want to give her any new hope.

"Stop it. Even Aunt Helga wasn't allowed to call me Stefan. I am flattered, Tilda, but Mik is waiting. We have a lot to do."

"Mik? Does that mean you have a mission from the architexter?" Her face showed genuine interest and approval. "Where to?"

"We decided not to tell anyone about our plans. This time Vist suggested investigating things in the old fashioned way."

"But you can tell me, Steve." Matilda put her hand on his chest and slowly slid it down. "You know me well, don't you?"

"I do, and that is why I won't say a word." Steven stepped back from the woman. "We broke up because you couldn't keep your mouth shut. Remember?"

"Oh yeah!" Matilda flushed in fury. "You loved my mouth as long as I didn't use it to speak!"

"Not true." Steven almost fell for this trick but stopped himself in time. He remembered that all he had to say had already been said once, and there was no need for repetition. "Please leave. I have only time enough to change my lock codes."

Matilda screeched, grabbed the glass of wine, and threw it into Steven's face. He dodged it quickly, which his enhancements enabled him to do. But the glass shattered against the wall behind him as he turned. Splashes of wine mixed with glass shards ricocheted across the left side of his face.

Matilda gasped and pressed both hands to her lips.

"I am so sorry!" she said in a very different voice, grabbing the serviette to wipe his blood off.

"Don't touch me!" Steven recoiled once again. "I can arrest you myself for trespassing and assault."

"What are those? Are they bad?"

"Go to the temple and check out Vist's 'New Additions to Law' offering. You will have to learn many new words if you do not want to join your father!"

"But Steven! I need to tell you something very important."

"What?" There was so much impatience and contempt in his voice that Matilda went pale and hurried out.

Steven went to the bathroom and squinted hard over the basin, squeezing out the bits of glass from his skin. Tiny special muscles in his dermis, a genetic borrowing from a local slug, contracted and pushed the glass out.

Steven treated his cuts and took a long gulp from the half-empty wine bottle.

Soon he joined Mik in the official conboat on their way to the riffs. Like all new Law Force vehicles, this one had been repainted in blue and yellow markings.

"I see you started already," Mik said, looking at his fresh wounds, "and we didn't even get there yet."

"Ha-ha, very funny. Congratulations, Mik, it was almost a joke," Steven said with a snort.

But Mik was dead serious. "Why you told me to bring a few ordermen with us?"

"I have a report from Danielle and her colleagues about this ritual on the island of Croc's Lips. Sura reported seeing a svoloch in this area.

What good would it be to make new rules and not follow them ourselves?"

"True."

"Do you fancy a walk there? Dani warned us that when the water rises, the island almost disappears below the surface. The moon here orbits slowly compared with Earth's Moon, but tides still occur."

"Sure," Mik said and added, after a few minutes of silence, "I assume you didn't cut yourself while shaving."

"No. Listen, Mik ... Do you have any more of that Caribs Estate Chardonnay?"

On arrival at Croc's Lips, Mik and Steven told the small group of armed city ordermen to stay on board while they looked for clues. Both stepped on the sand and found the beach well-washed by the waves and tide.

"As I suspected, we won't find anything. The water level is still dropping," Steven said and rubbed the back of his neck, feeling a migraine approach.

"Why is this series of islands called reefs? It's more like a row of volcanic rocks that stick out of the water."

"The reefs are further south. Croc's Teeth are the ones that stretch north. When the water level drops to low tide, it will be possible to walk through the mud from rock to rock."

"We might have to do that." Mik read the chemical detector, "Look, it's all the same and so full of sand and mica ... but there is a high concentration, a small trail. Almost like a beam."

"Where is it coming from?"

"Over there." Mik pointed at Croc's Teeth. Steven told the squad to wait for the signal and followed Mik, who went to the first fifteen-metre-high rock while still knee-deep in water.

At the eighth rock, they stopped. The water level dropped so much that the base of the "teeth" became visible. The grey and green mass of silt resembled the gums of those stone fangs and incisors. Mik and Steven checked this rock closely and soon found a bundle on a small ledge, too high to reach. Mik turned off the detector. The long, thin tentacle of Mik's third limb came out of his right shoulder pad. It easily reached the rock crevice, wrapped around the bundle, and pulled it out. The tentacle dropped an item into Mik's hands, then retracted back into his field suit's armour. The package was indeed small but heavier than it seemed at first glance. They both shuddered at the sight of something wrapped in a baby blanket, but inside was what they had hoped to find. It was the damned bluish totem.

"Vist was right. It's a device of some kind, but I can't read what it does. It must be my headache from today's accident," said Steven, rubbing his forehead.

"I had no accident, Steve," said Mik, "And my head is aching too."

"Really? Hang on – What's that?"

Both listened.

From the north side, along the row of "teeth," a rumble approached them, similar to the noise of a crowd. Both loaders simultaneously estimated the speed of approach, and decided not to wait for the unknown; they turned and hurried back to the Croc's Lip and the conboat.

Shiny and viscous silt mixed with fine sand tried to trap Steven's feet in its depths. Now his head ached so much that Vitr's light seemed almost as bright as the sun. He couldn't understand why Mik was running ahead as if he had a solid road under his feet. Steven gradually fell behind. A stone flew past Steven and plopped into the mud in front of him, spraying mud in all directions. And soon, a whole hail of large and small stones rained down around the loader. He looked back and saw a flock of creatures almost completely covered with hair approaching him from behind. They were closing in quickly and in synchrony, not so much running through the mud as jumping over nearly vertical walls of black stones. Svoloch! thought Steven in horror. Their agile bodies, reminiscent of apes, flew from rock to rock and jumped on the backs, shoulders and heads of those who ran in shallow water. At the same time, they made sounds that merged into one continuous roar. Steven had never seen anything like it. They were here weeks before their migration season, and they never appeared on the plain in such large groups. In the distance up ahead, he saw ordermen jumping out of the boat, activating zappers as they went to cover them.

Steven's head hurt like hell, and he thought he shouldn't have taken a sip of wine before going out.

Mik turned around and shouted something, but the roar was already so loud that Steven could only make out only the word "boots." He understood why Mik was running faster. His friend remembered to activate the scout power soles that Andrea had only recently perfected for situations like this. Steven was already reaching for the amulet with his finger, trying to formulate the command in his mind, but one of the stones hit his head, and he fell face down into the mud. By the time the first svoloch reached him, Steven could not feel his headache or hear the roar.

19. North

Even the fastest avion on Noverca flew very slowly compared with Earth aircrafts. There was no need for them to be fast yet since the colony was still small and had not yet left one continent. The only passenger flight from the capital flew to the city of Carib on Pettogreco in half an hour, and the researchers' cargo transports worked within the belt. The postal avions were all automatic, with a one-off ZPE charge one way. Therefore, the most distant expeditions were made on the old *Wasp*.

The last spaceship in the Wormhole Shift Perambulation (WSP) series was built on Earth. It travelled all over the solar system, performed multiple shifts through wormholes, and even came close to a black hole once.

Wasp always being on standby had its advantages. Even Obydva's craft, the fastest on Gera, couldn't cover the required distance in two hours. The other spaceships, recently built in the colony, were only intended for the one-time launch of satellites.

Nat had mostly good memories of *Wasp*. Now, he was her only pilot. He flew to the fallen transport's location with Obydva's precious cargo quite speedily in aircraft mode.

He loved these short adventures with Vist. Ever since he had returned from an expedition without Captain Tom Darkwood, he preferred to have the architexter always be part of the team. It was more reassuring that way.

"We are there," he said. "I'm going down."

In the seat next to him, Vist opened their eyes and said, "I looked again at the satellite images and compared the last one with the one before. There is a minimal difference of two hours between them. The body near the avion is no more."

"Covered with snow?"

"It hasn't snowed in the last two hours."

"So he got up and left?"

"That would only be possible if he were one of us. But even the tough nordians wouldn't have survived such a crash."

Nat checked the weather and said, "The wind is moderate. If the footprints are not covered, then we will find the guy."

Vist didn't answer this and closed their eyes again, then asked for something else from the satellite.

Nat landed so far from the avion that he did not disturb the snow near it. However, when both loaders arrived at the place, it turned out that the wind had swept away all traces outside the craft. But what they found inside confirmed that there was indeed someone in the automatic transport. It was also darker here than in Noverca's Comfort Zone, with the snow and ice glistening only in the light of the lantern on Nat's hazmat suit. Vist was relying only on their enhanced eyes even for greater distances. Vist wasn't wearing a survival suit, but their new thermoregulating hooded robe was as wide as a tent.

Inside the avion, without special lenses, nothing could be seen at all. On the autopilot's main programming panel, glass keyboards were smashed, wires pulled out, and navigation devices torn apart. It looked like a predator was tormenting it.

162

Nat picked up one of the pieces and sighed. "I guess this is not the nordian's handiwork unless he's gone crazy. Are these teeth marks? Has the svoloch done this?"

"It's possible. That would explain how it survived and recovered so soon. It must be alive because the satellite failed to find it again. Timofey couldn't even tell me whether it was alone or not. We won't find the creature in these conditions. The svoloch is too good at hiding, camouflaging, and masking its body temperature, and they also move very fast."

"Tell me about it. When we found the crater they were living in, it looked absolutely uninhabited from above. I almost flew in there."

"One cycle we might have to go there and take a closer look at that ship. But for now, it's their rightful reserve and sanctuary."

"How did this one manage to heal so fast without feeding?"

"It fed on Obydva's live cargo. Although I think most of the snowpillars escaped," said Vist and pointed back.

Nat looked around. A few plastic crates still full of porous dirty snow were scattered inside the craft and smashed. Most of them probably ended up outside in the snow when the avion fell.

Nat turned to Vist. "What do we do? Obydva lost his goods, the svoloch ran off, and the seismologists lost their transport. The computer has been torn apart. And there is still no communication with the station."

"No." Vist took off their backpack and opened it.

"We will have to fly to them and check," Nat said.

"Now we have to."

"Vist, are you *sniffing*?"

The architexter was indeed already holding the compound detector in their hands and muttered under his or her breath as if speaking out loud, "Maybe we should ask Viola to find a way to integrate the detector into our sensory system. If we can regulate it at will, we'll be able to perceive aromas to the extent we need. And imagine the delight—"

Vist stopped.

"Master?" Nat said, surprised by the look on the loader's face.

"Just in case, I wanted to determine the direction our saboteur had gone. But he left something more interesting behind here. Look at this, Nat."

A few holographic formulas appeared above the instrument in Vist's hands.

"This is mica," Nat said and felt his eyebrows rise too. "Blue salt? Here? So far from the crater?"

"Exactly. Let's go. Our presence at the station has become several times more necessary. I will report this find to Timofey on the way."

For the rest of the journey, Vist looked like a sleeping beauty on the passenger seat, but with a straight back and a slightly raised chin. Nat set the course further into the dusky darkness of the eternal winter and soon realised that finding the station was not easy. There were no lights on the landing site, no video or audio communication with the settlement, and even the automatic beacon was silent.

Wasp's scanners eventually found the station and landing site but chose only one platform suitable for parking. The sleeping beauty opened her eyes as soon as Nat shut down the engines. Vist's pupils were dilated to the limit, and their eyes looked black.

"Nat, be sure to take a zapper," Vist said in a male voice.

"I was about to suggest that myself." Nat waved his gloved hand. "But there doesn't seem to be anyone here. We don't need the rescue kits. The *Wasp* has not indicated any area where the temperature would be higher than minus forty-two. I don't sense anyone alive here."

Vist pulled the hood over their face and said, "You can always come back for those kits. Tell me, could the station's inhabitants possibly be buried deep in the ice in that large structure?"

"What structure?" Nat didn't understand, so he checked the results of the ship's mapper, "So that's why the *Wasp* was hesitant. They had another avion here ... and it fell through the ice. But why? And how?"

"We'll think about it," Vist said. "Let's not waste time."

The seismological stations were usually stretched in several directions like a snowflake with a power converter right in the middle. Vist went there first and discovered what the problem was. The ZPE power station was missing. The building was dead and didn't appear on the sensors as it had sustained significant damage inside and out. More than anything, it looked like a burgled house. The thieves had taken everything they found useful but left some electronic equipment, not all broken. Either they hadn't known what it was for, or it had become useless without a source of energy. Only one wing of the station was badly damaged. It looked crushed by a huge heavy object, and its end had fallen through the ice. All this had happened a long time ago because the water was frozen solid again and covered with thick snow. All the heat left the station through this wing, and snow blew into the corridors. Frost sparkled on the walls in the light of Nat's torches.

"Is there mica in here?" Nat asked when they had searched everything left of the station and found no people dead or alive.

"There is. Its concentration is higher in that direction." Vist pointed towards the snowy hills.

They walked towards them a few metres but saw nobody. However, Vist clearly sensed something.

"Nat, I can hear a pulse."

"A survivor?"

"No. Svolochs are coming. There are many, Nat." There was concern in the loader's voice.

"Well, we have nothing to fear from a few feral men," Nat said. "I am not afraid."

"Be afraid, Nat. Something is wrong – there are too many. Get ready to shoot. I'll take care of the *Wasp* and will be right back."

"What are you …?"

But Vist had already run back to the ship. Nat felt uneasy. The brave hunter listened and almost immediately heard a rumble and vibration in the ice mass. Thanks to Andrea's efforts, his shoes could replace seismologists' broken equipment if the need arose.

And then he saw the dark figures against the grey snow. A former hunter, Nat didn't need binoculars any more to see details far off. He squinted, zoomed in, and saw them.

Dozens of shaggy shapes ran down the slope against the grey background. They were naked, but their nakedness was covered by densely growing long hair on their backs and stomachs … It is easier to describe where this hair was not. But it was especially long and stiff on their head and shoulders, like a cat's whiskers. They ran quickly on two legs, strongly hunched over. Sometimes they helped themselves with their hands, pushing off the ice hills and, at the same time, advancing a couple of metres through a powerful acrobatic jump. Their heads bowed like a horse's, and their faces flashed with animal grins and the whites of their eyes. In their hands, they clutched short blades. At first, Nat couldn't decide if they were stone shards, broken bones or wooden stakes. But soon, he realised they were bits of metal, most likely originating from the thoroughly robbed station.

Nat grasped that when surrounded by these strange creatures, he would be torn to pieces in a matter of seconds. He clenched his left hand into a fist and raised it in front of him. Then he stretched his arm out in the svolochs' direction, and he activated the zapper with his thumb and slashed the ray across the crowd to the left and right.

The first rows of runners fell, decimated by a deadly, almost invisible beam. The dead tumbled forwards through inertia and lay still among the boulders. Nat hoped the others would come to their senses. After all, svolochs usually hide and attack people only if they come across their camp.

However, something strange was happening among the svoloch crowd. They kept coming in incredible numbers. At first, when the front runners fell, the others were clearly frightened. They ran slightly slower, bowing to the ground, hiding behind every snowy bump or rock. But when a whole avalanche of furry creatures flowed from behind the slope, it seemed that fear gradually left them. They moved faster, didn't pay attention to the fallen, and were already openly running towards death, jumping over the corpses, falling one by one.

And they became quieter too. Nat didn't hear the usual snarls, separate unintelligible words drawn out like groans or screams. Barely distinguishable faces took on the same expression, or rather its absence. All these ugly, overgrown faces turned into motionless masks, their eyes opened wide, filled with the same emptiness, and the long hair on the backs of their heads and shoulders stood on end.

Nat never suspected such determination in these timid and secretive creatures. But he didn't want to find out their objective. He mowed them down one by one, glad that the zapper's energy converter never lacked the long electromagnetic waves emitted by the red dwarf. But would Nat himself have enough strength?

At some point, the former hunter thought he was losing his mind. He saw those running in front suddenly take off into the air as if lifted by those behind them, but they continued to beat the air with their feet and were in no hurry to drop down. It was like something was holding them up by their backs. Nat then realised that it was the creatures themselves. Like ants clinging to each other, they had built a giant pyramid of constantly moving bodies. Nat had seen an anthill in Vist's garden, and what he saw here now made him think of it again. At first, the mass of hairy bodies was shapeless. It rippled and became denser. It reared in a wave and no longer looked like a crowd of bodies but like one huge shaggy creature with thousands of legs, arms and heads. And a second later, a real humongous monster rose in front of Nat. The hunter heard the growl again, but this time it sounded like the synchronised roar of a crowd escaping from the throat of one beast. A giant amoeba standing on its pseudopods, like a mammoth on its legs.

The severity of the strange phenomenon unexpectedly ended the attack, leaving a pile of corpses in its path. Apparently, the ice there was thinner, and the weight of the mutant crowd cracked it with a deafening sound. A lake of dark water formed between the svolochs and Nat. The ice that fell under the collective monster disappeared from sight, but several slabs immediately resurfaced, clean of the bodies.

Several creatures continued to run and fall into the water until a new strange thing happened. They all stopped as one. Some started shouting words and gesturing with their hands. They leaned towards the water and helped their fallen comrades to climb back onto the ice. Others simply turned around and trotted back up the icy slope. One or two even looked back at the station, squealed in confusion, and hurried away as quickly as possible.

Nat lowered his hands and looked at them in puzzlement. He felt his whole body tense. Terrible fatigue weighed him down like lead. When the last svoloch disappeared between the icy hills, Nat turned and walked back towards the ship, but then he stopped in his tracks. There was no *Wasp* at the landing site.

"Vist!" he shouted. The *Wasp*, just like the station craft and the synchronised svolochs, had gone under the ice, and the water was already solidifying above it.

With great effort, Nat forced himself to slow down, and he focused his thoughts on his amulet. He heard Vist's metallic voice in his earpiece, but it sounded like a broken record. Perhaps it was a record, as far as Nat knew.

"Tim ... Warmth ... Call"

For some reason, some words were missing, but those three words repeated with a significant gap between them. Vist could be trapped inside the *Wasp*, and something in the water may have interfered with the signal.

Tim? Of course. Nat could contact Timofey through the satellite too. He still had his amulet.

When he finished telling the architexter's purple apprentice about what had happened, he was unsure whether he had been coherent and brief enough. Still, Timofey responded as if he knew exactly what the problem was.

"Nat, do not waste time looking for Vist. I will contact Mik and send him on his way. Trust me, I will find the fastest avion on Gera. In fact, Obydva is still here. He might get to you in a cycle in his Bumblebag. You need to stay alive. Look for anything on the station made of carbon compounds. Nordians always keep enough pink wax in the service shed as emergency fuel for their transport. Lucky for you, they learned from their bad past experiences."

"I have my zapper."

"You need more energy than one zapper can provide. It will overheat and malfunction. You are further north, away from Vitr, but even our communication might drain your converter. Keep it for protection, so that you are able to defend yourself again. Vist told me you used to be a hunter on Earth and lived in the woods. Listen carefully and do what I say. You must find shelter and build a fire."

20. Gafan

The Great Martyr didn't know that one of her most devoted and obedient servants was watching her with great commitment. Gafan was not afraid that Morbus would discover him. He feared that one of the villagers would notice his efforts and report him to Morbus. Such an outcome could end in a slow and painful death for Gafan, if not worse. Or he would be questioned and would then get away. After all, although Gafan was not very smart, he surpassed any other villager in cunning, and not only in the Salty Village.

For a few cycles now, Gafan had noticed changes in the martyr's mood and behaviour. Morbus called the unfortunate victims to her bedroom less often. She was also less and less fussy about food and entertainment and paid less attention to the daily begging service. In addition, the service's quality and duration were no longer that satisfying to the villagers. Gafan was sure the villagers' trust in and admiration for Morbus were no longer the same. And only because they feared her wrath did they continue to work conscientiously in due subservience.

Gafan's life also changed. He had no more orders to go and meet with Karlina at the border posts to exchange contraband. Morbus had a new and very rich resource of sophisticated and necessary equipment. One cycle, Gafan woke up during one of the sleeping hours and watched how, very quietly, two strangers from their northern village brought two boxes containing something heavy to Morbus's house. The crates had an insulated coating on them, as if they had come from one of the research stations in the permafrost.

Rumours arrived from different villages, along with wagoners, about missing people and the unusual and untimely appearance in the forests of wild svolochs from the north. Gafan didn't believe it when someone recently noticed that a young woman named Melza had disappeared from their village.

It was no secret to anyone that a prisoner had been kept in the house of Morbus for over a month – that most recent new exile, whom Morbus hadn't accepted into the community. Why she didn't kill or kick him out, Gafan could only guess. After Morbus's experiment with Melza, he was sure that this prisoner and the appearance of strange idols wrapped in a rosary of blue crystals were connected. Gafan's last order was to go and hand over the first such item to Karlina, and Melza went with him more like an empty shell than a person.

A few cycles ago, Morbus also wore a new turban or helmet wrapped in cloth during the services. It looked heavy and was decorated with pieces of blue mineral. The villagers complained that they were losing their memory or that the devil was possessing them and forcing them to do ... Lord knows what. They pleaded to Morbus that she protect them, but she declared that a spirit did indeed have them – not a devilish one, but a divine one. Upon hearing this, Gafan became convinced that the blue crystal was to blame for everything and he called those cylindrical idols "possessors." He could never pronounce the name Morbus used.

Not all the villagers accepted that an angel possessed them. The belief began to grow among them that Morbus had made a deal with Satan and was selling him the souls of the exiled servants of the Lord.

One cycle Gafan decided that the whole thing would not end well for him or for Karlina. This happened when an old hunter was dragged from another village to be questioned by Morbus.

Terrible cries and pleas ceased only for the hour of sharing food, but none of the villagers had an appetite this time. They experienced nausea and some feral fear, accompanied by a massive headache.

Everyone tried to go about their business, but from time to time, they glanced towards the chambers of the Great Martyr. Gafan, whose house wasn't so far away from it, pretended to be digging in the garden, but he was, in fact, waiting for what would happen next.

The guard in front of Morbus's house stood as straight as his spear, which he held in the proper manner this time. Soon he was called in; he entered the house and immediately came out with the hunter's body thrown over his shoulder. He took a few steps and tossed the man with skin cut into ribbons into the dust of the square. Then he stood in his place, but even from a distance, Gafan could see the guard's legs shaking. His headache was gone, leaving only a dull discomfort behind his ears. The disturbed chickens ran off to the side but soon returned as if nothing had happened.

Behind Gafan, a neighbour appeared with a basket full of weeds. Gafan glared at her and turned to see whether the man on the ground would move.

"Who was that?" the old woman asked softly. She smiled nervously, and the white clay on her face was covered in small cracks.

"Ahiga, a travelling hunter," Gafan replied without turning around.

"Looks like he shared a great burden of suffering with our martyr. But what for, do you know?"

"I don't know," Gafan lied. He knew well that the hunter had really let Morbus down. Even remembering his own summons in the big house with Morbus made the old scars on his back burn.

"It doesn't matter," the neighbour continued. "Looks like the burden of the Great Martyr is so heavy that it had to be shared. What a great blessing! I hope this man's suffering is over, and now he is walking hand in hand with our Lord, along the rays of the blessed Vitr—"

"Shut up, old crow!" said Gafan, hissing. He felt sick again after her words.

The older woman disappeared and was soon replaced by her husband, a bony-looking man in a grey knitted kilt.

"Hey, Gafan, did he move yet?"

Gafan turned to face the man. "No. I think he is gone. Do you know where his possessions are? He had no property in our village but would have carried a bedroll or something."

"A bedroll?" the bony neighbour rubbed his chin, "You might be right. If he had one, it would be in the house. I will ask the guard."

"Yeah, you do that, and I will see if I have anything to wrap him into if he has lost his things."

Gafan tapped his shovel on a piece of rock to clean it, then he entered his house. It was more of a shack than a house. The interior looked more like a pantry, full of baskets, boxes and bags. In the corner behind the door lay a mattress stuffed with dry grass and a flat stone that served as a table. Gafan looked around the room, then he put down his shovel, opened one of the crates, and carefully examined several knitted bedspreads and rugs. He chose the holiest and oldest spread, picked up a shovel, and left the house.

On the square in front of the house of Morbus, about four people were already standing near the guard, busily rummaging through the dead hunter's travel bags.

Gafan walked over and turned the corpse face up. Glassy eyes stared up at the sky with inhuman agony. Gafan lowered the dead man's eyelids with his hand and spread a rag on the ground.

"Help me," he called to the guard, but the guard just shook his head, silently clutching his spear. Gafan noticed the dusty paths left by the streams of urine on his left leg.

A skinny neighbour pulled the hunter's leather vest over his naked torso and grabbed the dead man by the ankles, helping Gafan roll the body onto a rag.

One of the villagers had already tucked a good-quality sleeping bag under his arm that may have once belonged to a country patrol or a geological scout. But Gafan pulled the roll from him and said firmly and adamantly, "Don't even think about it if you don't want to be left without a decent grave yourself. A man has the right to his last bed."

The villager didn't argue, and soon Gafan carried a shovel on his shoulder and dragged that sleeping bag along the ground, on which lay a body tightly wrapped in an old rag soaked with blood.

The skinny neighbour walked beside him and occasionally helped if there was an obstacle in the way, such as a stone or a hole. He couldn't stop talking, "He said ... you know ... he said the Great Martyr was angrier than usual. The job was not done, yes. Although that was half the trouble. You could always make another attempt. But the girl ran away. You know, that pretty one ... her favourite cleaner. So it was necessary to take out the anger on someone. It's good that the hunter was caught. Otherwise, one of us would have to pay for her sin."

Gafan remained silent, thinking about some issues of his own and how Morbus had gone berserk lately. He didn't believe in all this nonsense about sharing the burden and divine duty. If before, on a whim, Morbus used to summon an unfortunate villager or a passing tramp once a month, now half the village walked around with bruises, burns and monstrous cuts. One guy had never left his shack after he and his wife had been forced to share the bed with the martyr. The man's wife went to the northern caves for ice daily, and Gafan was sure they will have no more children.

The village cemetery was not far away, in the dunes above the sea. Instead of tombstones, there were low pyramids made of salt spheres.

Gafan told his neighbour to go down to the beach and bring exactly ten balls approximately the same size but no smaller than his head. Several trips should be enough. He began to dig. The sand was damp and heavy, so it didn't crumble back into the shallow grave.

Gafan decided he needed to talk with Karlina. If the young cleaner-girl was not found soon nearby or in the neighbouring villages, she must be in the city. The sooner Karlina would help to bring her back, the more villagers, including Gafan himself, would remain intact.

The skinny neighbour dragged up the first two balls and sat down to rest and chat. "And there is also such news from our fisherman's brother. The Great Martyr ordered one of the collectors of coastal snails to look for signs of the appearance of a wildmen. As soon as traces of the camp are found or their song heard, the collector must make it known right away. Do you suppose Morbus wants to catch one?"

"What for?" Gafan stopped digging. "That's all we needed."

"Don't ask me. Whatever the Lord's wish ... but if we cage the wildman, can you imagine what Morbus will feed it with?"

"No. I don't even want to think about it."

"My point exactly. Everyone knows the svoloch eat one another or anyone."

When the grave was ready, Gafan put the bedroll at the bottom and carefully lowered the hunter on it, in a sleeping position, on his side. A neighbour knelt next to the grave with his palms together and moaned in a high voice. Gafan stopped him. "It's okay; you don't have to. I will beg for his soul myself. Go home. Tell your wife that you worked hard and deserved a whole tock from my share."

The bony neighbour was happy to leave. Gafan waited for a minute, absorbed in deep thought, and then pulled the bedroll from under the body. He covered the hunter with sand and built the pyramid. Then he came to another grave that was different from the rest. Its pyramid was made of a few round stones instead of spheres. Gafan picked one of the stones and turned it over in his hand. It was not a stone but the empty shell of a coastal slug, almost indistinguishable from large pebbles. Gafan took out a beautiful brooch with two fingers from the cavity of the shell and lifted it to Vitr's light to charge. Soon above the brooch, a screen the size of a palm rose. The face of Matilda Crossich appeared in it.

Gafan laughed happily. "I started to worry that this amulet was no longer working," he said, sighing in relief, "I'm so glad to see you, my girl!"

"Dad? What's happened?"

"This happened. I miss you."

"But this connection is only for urgent news. You are lucky that I am home alone."

"So I have a lucky cycle. Where is Karlina?"

"Mum works in the store. She bought sugar at a good price."

"That's wonderful. We do have an urgent matter, though. You must find someone in the city for Morbus and use the possessor to cross the borders."

"Oh, I really don't want to. We have only one left, and I don't want Morbus to use it on me. See the scar? She did this to me, and Steven doesn't find me pretty any more."

"You are the prettiest of all. One is enough, and it's not you who would 'act' for the martyr. Listen to me carefully. I will show you where to put it ..."

21. The Permafrost

Old Marta's avion Bumblebag was a truly hideous craft, one of the first Rod Baker built with Novercian engineers about fifty years ago. It was noisy and had uncomfortable seats, but it was still reliable and easy to maintain. Obydva used it as his personal interurban transport. This time he navigated to the north just above the smooth layer of cantaloupe clouds, so low that a narrow strike of shadow from the aircraft directly ahead was visible.

He sat in the pilot's seat, but for many years there had been no wheel at the control column and no buttons, toggle switches or indicators in front of him. Even the screen had been raised for Mik's sake this time. The tall back of the chair was the point of contact between the vessel's control and the loader's perception. However, Obydva had the same focused and calm expression on his face as any other ordinary pilot.

"I thought you left it for Nat to inherit," said Mik, trying to adjust the seat without breaking it.

"Well, I changed my mind. I told him that since I was not dead after all, I needed it for myself. He didn't mind at all. Such a good boy! How was your nap, Mik?"

"Are you joking?"

"No. You used to be able to sleep on the sharp rocks of Devil's Bay during the storm. What happened to you?"

"I still can sleep on the sharp rocks of Devil's Bay during the storm. I could never sleep here and I never would. Are we there yet?"

"Almost. We have no direct connection with the temple any more, but the satellite signal is fine. I guess any minute now" – a long beep announcing the approach to the target interrupted him – "we'll hear Mr Alloway's beacon. Time to land."

The engines' roar slightly changed, and the Bumblebag dived into the gentle clouds ungracefully, briefly breaking their ideal smoothness.

It took another hour or so before they found the station by a single speck of heat on the energy screen.

"Don't land on the ice. Timofey understood from Nat's words that at least two patches of ice had been broken under the weight of something. The *Wasp* went down, but Tim didn't understand much about the second one."

Obydva nodded, probed the nearest ridge of rocks, and pointed at the map screen.

"This area is the safest. A bit far from the station, but I have a luge."

"You have a *what*?"

"A sort of snowmobile, called a convluge. Steven built it for me when I had just started harvesting a little nix for my research. Didn't he show it to you?"

"I remember now. I thought he built them to take ladies for a ride. It was the year he switched from old cars to snowmobiles and yachts until he got bored even with them."

"What does Steven reinvent nowadays?"

"Scooters or mopeds. Much more popular among young people. He calls them conbikes."

Obydva's smile melted away. "I hope he will be all right after that attack."

"Well, you know Steve. No adventure is complete for him without bandages and hospitals. He's had worse in the past, and now he's a loader. Will be up in a cycle or two."

"Sometimes I suspect he ends up in the hospital because Zina takes care of him personally there."

Mik checked the distance between their landing point and the station. "And why did the nordian seismologists build a station on the ice?"

"It's almost as old as this ship. Back then, apparently, the ice was thicker, and it was more expensive to build on these vertical stones."

"I see. And they only had one avion?"

Obydva thought for a moment. "There were two. I remember now. Definitely two."

"One crashed. Where is the second one?" Mik lifted his eyes to the screen again as the Bumblebag flew over the establishment.

"Good question. Nat! Nat! Are you there?" Obydva said out loud. After a short pause, he added, "Mik, he answered. Prepare for landing."

The clumsy-looking avion landed on a rocky slope at an angle of thirty-seven degrees without a single jolt. The jagged legs, bent and pressed, now unfolded. They affectionately clasped the granite and fixed their position so that even a quake wouldn't be able to shake the avion off the rock. The engine stopped, and there was complete silence. Obydva relaxed and got up from his chair. "Ready?"

"You are still the best pilot I know," said Mik, breathing again.

"But you can drive terrestrial vehicles better than me. I highly recommend you have a go on the luge. We have to dress for minus fifty-one degrees Celsius. Shall we?"

Soon, from the open hatch in the Bumblebag's "thorax," a retractable tunnel stretched to the ground like a long and winding spyglass. Then it spat out the convluge and pulled back. When driving across the snowy desert, Mik wasn't the kind of person who would shout "woo-hoo!" easily, but he was pretty close to doing that. The luge flew across the snow, and only a very miserable person driving it would not wish the journey to be twice as long. Unfortunately, concern for Nat's and Vist's safety clouded the fun that Mik and Obydva experienced.

Mik stopped the luge in front of a heavily insulated but empty flat building. Soon, Obydva and Mik discovered what Vist and Nat had found earlier. Mik pointed to the column of smoke rising from the station's south-west wing, which looked less damaged. Obydva confirmed that this was also Nat's location, and they went straight to him with the rescue kit. A little while later, they knocked on the room door and heard Nat moving something behind it before opening it.

The room was small and full of smoke from a fire in a hastily built stove. Nat had made it from concrete debris and panels torn from the walls. Some pieces of furniture, garbage and something else were burning in the stove, which made even the loaders pinch their noses.

Nat himself couldn't smell it. He was fully dressed in his special suit Andrea had made, with a helmet full of thermal and chemo-filters, and he was breathing air pumped from the outside straight into the filters through a hose.

When Mik finished putting out the fire, he aired the room, and asked. "Have you set up a crematorium here? Whose remains are you burning? Station dwellers?"

Obydva had already given Nat something to drink, recharged his suit heater, and removed his helmet. But Nat's eyes closed and he answered with a barely moving tongue, "And them too. There was nothing but bones. I found them by luck. I searched for everything that burns. Timofey's instructions—"

"And why didn't you recharge your suit with the zapper's converter? You know the scout rules. You've only achieved a few extra degrees here with this fire."

"I only have one. Vist has another. I didn't know how long I would have to wait. And the communication ... And if they return ..."

Obydva checked Nat's vital readings. "Mik, his core temperature is 34.9°C, and I urgently need to take him to the avion. I'm not a doctor, but it seems that if we had arrived a couple of hours later, it would have been too late. If it weren't for his implants, he would have died by now."

"But where's Vist, Nat?"

Nat closed his eyes again. "I'm so tired. Searched everywhere for carbon. Wasp ... under ..."

Obydva glanced briefly at Mik. "Look for Vist without me. I'll be back soon." He lifted Nat in his arms effortlessly and carried him to the sleigh. "Hold on, son. We'll be home soon."

22. Zina

Steven was conscious for almost an hour but was in no hurry to let the Black woman sitting next to his bed know about it. Zina sat, turned away a little, and read something from her amulet's small holo-screen. Steven noticed the long braid over her shoulder had gotten thinner and whiter since she last nursed him back to health. When was that? Oh yes. Straightaway after his implantation surgery and uploading. So almost twenty years ago. But how beautiful she is still. She has not lost her royal posture, although her waist is no longer so thin. After what happened to Tom, she also agreed to become a loader. Steven was pleased with her decision, but not because it preserved her beauty. He was happy that she would live a long and healthy life. Her eye colour changed, her lameness disappeared, and she became much calmer. Now the concern for patients on her face was not accompanied by anxiety, and her house was again filled with beautiful things and guests.

He has long come to terms with the fact that his love will never be returned. But he saw his most cherished desire before him whenever he found himself like this ... alone with Zina in the same room. Steven allowed himself to admire her profile a little more and coughed with restraint.

"Finally," Zina said in her velvety voice, not looking up from her reading, "How is my most regular patient doing?"

"Hungry," Steven said with a playful growl.

"I warn you right away that there are no grilled beetles. They're in short supply now."

"What? No sandies? Put me back into a coma," Steven said and lifted his hand to his bandaged head.

"Don't touch it," Zina said seriously. She deactivated the holo-screen and turned to face him. "Your skull was cracked open, remember? This time, you are growing horns."

"I am?"

"Absolutely," her look became sly.

"In that case, may I have beef meatballs with mash and Obydva's tock sauce and gherkins? Do we still have any? How long was I out this time?"

Zina ordered the meal and glanced at Steven's badge on the side table, "Since the operation? Six hours and forty-four minutes. Excluding the time you spent staring at me."

"Oh no! Ten minutes and I would have beaten my own record!"

"Ten minutes? Over or under?" Zina asked and got up to get him a dressing gown.

Steven thought for a moment. "I don't remember. Hey! Doesn't matter."

He sat up as the nurse entered the room with a tray. Zina pulled the long tabletop from the wall and said to Steven, "Careful, you will be healing until next cycle's lunchtime. Try not to move fast and—"

"I know, meine Dame." Steven put the dressing gown on and, before eating a mouthful, asked, "So what happened to us on the shore? Is Mik okay? Did anybody else get hurt? Do you know what was wrong with the svoloch? Is Vist back yet? What was that blue thing?"

"Slow down, so many questions! Mik and Obydva went to join Vist and Nat in the north. The last time I heard from Timofey, he assured me he would keep us updated. The svoloch that attacked you ran off as soon as they injured you when Mik and his ordermen scared them off. No one else was hurt." Zina hesitated and watched Steven chewing on his food. "The blue artefact is in the temple, being studied. Or what's left of it, at least. All I did was a full bio-analysis, but there is only Mik's DNA on it and that of the creatures he hit with it." She sighed. "What else? Oh, yes. The most important thing! Since Mik and Vist are both away, it is up to you to talk to a messenger from the village. She is with Scarlett now, getting a full physical and psychological examination."

"What messenger?" Steven almost choked on his food.

"A teenage runaway who came back from the village. According to the new legislation, she is entitled to medical help, but after hearing the girl out, the ordermen brought her to Kinghall instead of sending her right back out."

"Why?"

"She said she knows about the fire in the capital and must talk to General King. At least, that's what the border guards understood. Mik is away.

They contacted Grand, but the girl refused to speak to him and asked for a specific audience. Grand contacted me."

"Am I fit enough to go to Kinghall?" Steven left the fork on the plate and glanced at the bed monitor.

"Sure. Just take care. I will come with you if you want."

Steven smiled and winked. "As my date? Yes, please."

"I changed my mind."

"As an escort, then?"

"Go to hell."

"As my wife?"

An awkward silence filled the room. Both looked at the nurse, who was still standing by the door. She was a young terrenian earthling with huge eyes. She looked at them with a childish simplicity and excitement as if watching a film. When her eyes met Zina's, she nodded fervently, then mumbled an apology and ran out of the room.

"What's her name?" Steven asked.

"This was Nurse Ayo. She's my most nosy. Your type?"

"I'm talking about the village girl."

"Melza, daughter of Naria Senkuvene from Senkus farm. Scarlett has already reported to me that apart from being undernourished, she is not only quite healthy but also doesn't show signs of violence or of physical violation, which is so common in the wildlands. Very odd."

"All things have gotten very odd lately," Steven said as he got up and walked over to the mirrored alcove where his clothes were. "Zina, Tom is gone. Are you really going to live alone forever now? Despite all the banter, you know I never joked about my feelings for you."

He opened the closet, took off his gown, and turned away from Zina to show her his powerful back with white-but-suntanned, very earthly skin covered with numerous scars, burns and stitch marks from many decades of adventures. Steven saw her in the mirror. She turned away towards the holographic window and switched on the video landscapes in his image collection.

"Don't tell me you were serious about them either," she said angrily. She found an image of a maple park in autumn and stopped, following the raindrops on red leaves with her eyes.

"Why not? I was more than serious."

"You dated more women than there are blobsters in the ocean."

"Not until after you married Tom," Steven grumbled as he put on his shoes.

"You knew it wasn't a valid marriage. Not at first, anyway."

Steven stood up, fully dressed now. His face was red in frustration. "Oh yes. Let me remember what it was at first. You were both smitten with Vist but couldn't have her. How did you expect me to handle it?" he walked over to Zina and changed the screen from autumn to a French cabaret, where several beauties kicked their perfect legs up high. "I tried to talk to you, but you didn't want to know."

"We were all living in abnormal conditions. How come Mik didn't get so desperate? And Steven, it was a very long time ago."

"Exactly. Now you blame me for trying to move on with my life? Just don't compare me to Mik. He's different. I tried to match him with the best people I could think of. I needed you, so I strained to—"

"I am trying to move on too." Zina turned to Steven with wet eyes. "I will be a grandmother next year."

"And I am older than General Lillipond was when he died of old age. Zina, we are not the same people. We have changed in many ways our parents couldn't imagine. People change. Their values change with them. You see it every few years. Sometimes one day can change everything. It can change you beyond recognition."

"I definitely don't remember you ever speaking in such a way back on Earth. Have you finally grown up by the age of ...?"

Steven gently put his finger over her lips.

"Shh, I am flattered that you counted my birthdays, but I didn't, so it's better not to know. Shall we?" He gestured towards the door.

Zina finally smiled a little. "Aren't you going to ask me to think about it?"

"What for? We are on Noverca, in the O'Teka colony. Thinking is happening all the time here."

A few hours later, after finishing his conversation with Melza, Steven asked to meet Grand in person and petitioned for Melza's official pardon because of her invaluable service to O'Teka. At first, Melza refused to speak with them, saying she was told to meet with a brown-skinned officer. Zina stepped in and asked, looking directly into her eyes, "Am I brown enough?" After this, the girl agreed to talk about recent events in the Salty Village. Her mother was notified. Zina and Scarlett took the girl to stay at her poultry farm until the final decision. Steven requested from the temple all materials on the communication scientist Davon Marchel. Then he went home, locked all the doors, and spent the rest of the cycle in his workshop. He was inspired, serious ... and very happy. Zina agreed to a date in his yacht. He had dreamed of this for many generations.

23. Mik

Obydva left with Nat strapped to the back seat of the convluge. Mik connected his amulet to the detectors and went through the station looking for Vist, for *Wasp*, and for any clue that could help him.

He started with the building and found what used to be a medical facility stripped of all things that were not attached to the floor. Like an examination bed, for example. Mik set up the portable ZPE unit to warm the room up, unpacked the rescue kit, and sealed the room with a power field. If he were to find Vist alive, he would bring them here. If not, he may need this room for himself after a few hours. Unlike Nat, he had everything necessary to survive while waiting. It was a shame

Nat wasn't in a state to say more, but he had said enough to Timofey earlier.

Mik went to where the *Wasp* was supposed to be when they landed a cycle ago. The craft's landing spot was almost levelled under new snow, but a shard of ice here and there indicated that the ice was broken, and that the chunks had floated on the briefly exposed water before freezing again.

The loader's scanner couldn't miss large objects, but it seriously struggled with smaller signals, and something in the ice was jamming it. Mik scanned the area for large masses of metal and immediately confirmed that the old spaceship was frozen motionlessly about fifteen metres under the surface. That is what Nat had tried to say.

Fifteen metres was nothing. They had pulled plenty of evacuation pods in the past from even deeper ice, although no vessels this big.

A few paces away from the submerged *Wasp*, another large object was trapped in the ice. Mik scanning it for its shape and realised he had found the second avion belonging to the unfortunate nordians. What had happened here? Why had they fallen under the ice? The temperature here hardly changed, and so the ice's upper layer shouldn't weather. Might the integrity of the ice have been compromised by the water temperature below the ice? Or by vibrations? And where was Vist? Gone?

Was it even possible that Vist might die? Mik felt a sudden, acute pain over the potential loss of the architexter. He had never really cared about what might happen to Vist because Vist always seemed indestructible and always knew the right thing to do.

Mik walked around the station's entire territory and the nearby sites with installations, but his amulet in his head circlet didn't catch a living heartbeat. He reassured himself that with Vist, it just didn't mean anything ... but more than a cycle had passed since Nat had lost the architexter. Where could Vist be, then? They had left Nat to repel the attack of the svolochs while she had to protect the Wasp. And then the ship fell through the ice. There was no way Vist could not have predicted this possibility because he was not a bungler and should have learned by then about the second avion.

Mik's thoughts swirled like a tornado. How could Vist protect the Wasp from a crowd of svolochs? After all, judging by the destruction at the station, they could pull the ship apart. What would Mik himself do in Vist's place? Well, of course!

He returned to the place where the Wasp was buried and scanned the ice metre by metre, searching for Vist's amulet. It was most likely deactivated, but the satellite beacon should make itself felt from time to time. How often, Mik couldn't know. Vist's amulet was different from all the others.

Mik turned to the satellite and called Timofey.

Vist's apprentice confirmed that the signal was being picked up. "A message too – just three words every few minutes," Timofey said. "It was meant for Nat's earpiece, but it's coming from where you're standing ... the radius is no more than two metres."

Mik fell to his knees, shovelled the snow, and activated the zapper. He melted the first few centimetres of ice to make it more transparent while sending a bright beam of light into the thick ice.

After only a few minutes, he saw what he hoped to see. Less than half a metre from the surface, a cocoon of ucha-silk was frozen in the ice.

Carefully, trying not to hit the loader, Mik cut out a conical piece of ice with a zapper and quickly, before it froze in again, he picked it up with a power anchor and dragged it onto the snow. He caught his breath and thanked his artificial muscles for their superhuman strength.

He chiselled off as much ice as possible, lifted the remaining chunk on his shoulder, and carried the whole piece into the previously warmed room like a boulder.

He carefully placed the ice on the bed to examine it, but then he realised that he didn't know what to do next. If one of his scouts had been here in place of Vist, then without the slightest doubt, he would have set to work tirelessly. But Vist wasn't a colonist with a handful of implants. This complex and numerously reborn creature could react unexpectedly to a simple routine.

Water dripped from a solid and shapeless bundle of grey fabric. It became softer before Mik's eyes, and its rubbery folds began to unravel and sag. It reminded Mik of a slowly blossoming bud for an unimaginable flower or a chrysalis of a giant insect that had come back to life.

Mik stood over Vist and said with a deep sigh, "I guess you were a little late, mate. You didn't surface fast enough. The ice froze faster. You drowned the Wasp on purpose, didn't you? Tell me, can the famous loader survive almost thirty hours in a freezer?"

The wet fabric sagged and clung to the loader. Soon Mik saw the shape of a motionless figure on its side in a foetal position.

Mik's thoughts made him ache, and his chest felt tight. Mik was not used to such feelings. He never thought about who Vist was to him, and he found relating to others even harder. He knew for himself that loaders are capable of relationships. General King had many friends and loved his colleagues and students. He felt very strongly about the death of Tolyan and Marta. Mik cared about what happened to Tom; even Harlow's death caused painful sadness. But he never allowed himself to feel anything like what he experienced by Vist's side in this frozen and deserted station. And what, in fact, had he always felt about Vist?

"Nothing unreasonable," he said aloud.

There are things that people don't know about themselves. Loaders know more. When Mik agreed to prolong his life and lie on the operating table in the architexter's house, he knew he trusted Vist completely. Now he was a loader too. He decided to limit himself to only physical improvements, as Steven, Nat and even Zina had. But then it turned out that he was more self-aware than ever. It became more difficult for him to convince himself despite the facts. He now cared even less about how others saw him, and during their meetings, he sat in a dark corner more out of habit than out of need.

A wet sleeve slipped off Vist's face, and Mik saw a strand of hair stuck to a pale cheek. Tears filled Mik's eyes. Too late. The skin was white, with a slight blue tinge. It looked dead, but Vist's robe was still doing its job. Something inside the bio-suit turned itself on, and Mik heard a rustling sound within the fabric. He knew that was a drying mechanism that had just joined the heater.

Mik carefully placed his hand on the ice-cold forehead and realised that he had never touched Vist before. He tried to remember at least a handshake and failed. He remembered their first meeting on the Mars orbit. He really hadn't liked Vist at that point. He had been unable to forgive the loader for losing two of his comrades that day. Then he couldn't help but respect Vist, not so much for what the loader did to save humanity, but for how Vist handled things, people and himself. Or herself. Mik thought again about how he never cared whether Vist was a man or a woman. He disapproved of Tom's obsession with Vist in the distant past, Zina's devotion, Rod's suspicions, General's constant astonishment, Steven's curiosity and even Tolyan's indifference ... and Marta? Marta had also respected Vist. Mik couldn't recall what Chang used to think.

Now Mik cared. He really cared for Vist's survival too. Mik quickly took his hand off Vist's head. He was sure he felt something different in Vist's cold flesh. But what? An involuntary muscle contraction? An electric impulse? The robe was already dry inside and out. Vist's skin too. Light plumes of steam gradually rose from the wet hair, together with an almost imperceptible smell. It wasn't the smell of death. Mik's nose greedily breathed in the scent of honey wax. He pressed his fingers to Vist's neck and held his own breath.

A pulse! It was a very slow pulse but regular enough to be unmistakable. Mik searched through his pockets and fished out his light-intensifying glasses. He saw what he hoped to see when he took it closer to Vist's lips. Vist was breathing. But only just.

"Come on, loader!" Mik called out, "Warm up!"

Why so slowly? Something wasn't working. Vist somehow managed to preserve their life but could still die if the suit malfunctioned. Mik decided to apply his scout methods now. He pulled blankets from the rescue kit, arranged them on the floor, grabbed Vist under the armpits, and pulled the loader down from the medical bed into a sitting position on the blanket. Vist's body was already limp, their heavy head falling to their knees. The room was slowly filling with steam like an industrial laundrette. Mik put the warming gloves on and turned the heaters up. He knelt behind Vist, pushed aside the robe's hood, and found the fastener. It didn't even cross his mind that he was about to see what no one else had ever seen. Not once. Vist's naked back and shoulders.

Mik pressed his hands into the white skin and felt how cold it was, even through the warm gloves. But he also felt rib cage movements. And he heard a quiet cough, followed by a full but wheezy inhalation. Mik took the gloves off and threw them away.

"Oh! Forget the dammed routine! This isn't quick enough!"

Mik's dark hands looked even darker against Vist's skin. He started to rub the icy back and upper arms. It felt like he was trying to melt snow, but Vist was alive, that was all that mattered. Even more so as Vist lifted their head and threw it back. Their olive eyes opened and stared up straight into Mik's eyes. Mik looked down and thought the loader was trying to say something.

"What was that?" he asked, leaning closer.

Vist wheezed, "Too ... seriously ..."

"I know, I know. Tell me what I can do."

"Never ... had to ..." and then the voice died out, and Vist's bluish eyelids closed again.

Mik didn't understand but trusted his gut. It took him less than a minute to get rid of his hazmat suit. The buttons of his favourite old shirt flew in all directions, and he pressed his hairy chest against the loader's bare back. He rubbed Vist's shoulders and arms with his palms until they felt warmer. He avoided Vist's chest just in case or instinctively. Vist's heart rate increased, but their lungs stopped making a wheezing noise. Mik panicked. Was Vist not breathing any more? He cupped the loader's face with one hand, drew in a full chest of air, and pressed his mouth against Vist's thin lips.

24. Poultry Farm

Melza lay on a bed in the spacious room she had known all her life. This room was a nursery, an extension to the house her grandfather built. And Melza lived in it until she was fourteen years old. When she ran away from home, she was sure her parents would find new uses for the space.

Now she looked at her simple furniture, her things, the holograms on the ceiling, and the walls, wondering why all this had remained untouched for almost two years. She thought about her school friend who was attacked by a swarm of goon-flies during the expedition and didn't survive. The goon-fly victim's parents didn't change his room either, knowing he would not return. Of course, Melza's mother had more reasons to hope.

At the start of the last cycle, when she and her parents arrived at the farm, she took a long bath to scrape off the white clay and salt of the accursed village. Then her mother led her to a mirror in a brightly lit room with huge windows. Melza was astonished. She hadn't seen herself in such a long time. She forgot the colour of her eyes and how her washed skin shimmered in the red rays of Vitr. Her ashen hair, which she always gathered in a bun at the back of her head and tied with a rag, grew long and now flowed over her shoulders like a waterfall. She wanted to cry with joy at how much she looked like her mother.

"Look at us, daughter. We are strong and capable and can do much for the colony and ourselves. I'm so glad you're back to O'Teka ... in every way. Your life will have purpose again," her mother said.

Melza shuddered when she first heard the word "purpose." After all, it meant responsibility, creativity, commitment, study and work. But she didn't forget about her life in the village so soon. She had to work harder than ever there, constantly worried about her failure to please others and always afraid of the Great Martyr. There was no development, achievement, pride and definitely no fun. Finding the right purpose gave you all that.

Fun! Melza got up and, still wearing her pyjamas, rushed out of the house. The smell of her favourite crunchy waffles from the kitchen nearly made her change course, but she decided they weren't going anywhere. Her desire to experience fun again was stronger.

She ran barefoot through a rust-coloured flower garden, where tall flowers with the strange name "sunflower" bowed their huge heads. Melza tore off one petalless mature disc, then hurried towards a long low building, in front of which pockmarked large crimson birds roamed over a wide yard. They raised their heads, and when they saw Melza with a sunflower in her hands, they flapped their wings and cackled. They quickly surrounded her, and Melza began to pull out fistfuls of seeds and scatter them around.

The large silver-laced caperturkeys pecked and quarrelled, and Melza couldn't help but laugh wholeheartedly. She was a child again, and the same pride that she was doing a useful thing and getting pleasure from it overwhelmed her.

When she ran out of seeds, Melza entered the coop and went to the conveyor belt, collecting eggs that had fallen on it from the elevated nests. The eggs were different sizes, and Melza chose the largest, the size of a teacup, dark and speckled. She shook it for a minute, holding it with both hands, then made two holes in the shell and drank the contents with delight.

A sudden and familiar headache spoiled this sensation, but the girl didn't have time to acknowledge it. A big brown cat, quietly watching Melza from the top of the control panel, suddenly opened his eyes wide and hissed at her. The empty eggshell fell out of Melza's hands and cracked. The girl turned and walked awkwardly towards the exit. As if blind, she walked hard into the frame, but instead of crying out in pain, she swore under her breath in one of the dead languages. Blood poured from a cut eyebrow and flooded her left eye, but Melza didn't wipe it off or even raise her hands. She stumbled to the farm gate, not along the path, but straight through corn and wet moss fields. Slashed by sharp leaf blades and with numerous cuts on her legs, she went to the gate and put her hand on the lock panel.

About a hundred metres from the entrance, a man with a face smeared with clay and dressed in a knitted tunic approached her. Beside him was the village forager's wheelbarrow. "Your greatness. There are many goods on the farm. While the gates are off, we could get plenty of—"

The girl interrupted him with a frozen face and strange voice. "Don't you dare! I'll rip your hands off. There's a bio-alarm on every farm. They'll notice quickly and catch up even quicker. Can you tell me what a waffle is?"

With these words, Melza woke up and gasped. But the man in the tunic, whom she immediately recognised as Gafan, hit the girl in the face, put her in a wheelbarrow, and rolled her towards the sea, avoiding the roads.

25. Ganda

Vist survived the ice? Wow! As soon as Obydva got the message, he rushed back to the station. He had so many questions for the architexter! When he got off his luge, he found Vist in the first aid room, wrapped in brightly coloured emergency blankets and holding a mug of steaming broth with both hands. The room was hot like a sauna; Mik had raised four holo-screens in the dark far corner, where he carefully studied pictures taken from the satellite while sweating in his survivor's suit.

Besides the heat, a strange, awkward atmosphere hung in the air.

"Is everything okay?" asked Obydva and took a step towards Vist to take them by the hand, but Vist moved the mug away firmly.

"I am alright, Obydva. Mik saved my life. Everything he did for me was very timely."

Obydva turned to Mik, but his friend just sat there with a stiff back.

"Better tell us more about Nat and what he saw," Mik said.

"Nat didn't get frostbite and, to my great relief, will be as good as new pretty soon. He took a warm bath, ate, and is now sleeping. Vist, it would be better for you to follow his example. He still hasn't added anything to the description we already received from Timofey. Do you still associate what happened here with what happened in the city?"

Mik stood up and slowly walked over to Obydva. "The death of the station's inhabitants, your crashed cargo and the crimes in the colony are connected. Therefore, we must do more work here before returning home."

"I'll add that we're missing important evidence worth looking for here." Vist put the mug down on the floor and stood, still wrapped from head to toe in blankets.

Obydva noticed that the famous robe was lying on the floor, but now was not the time to be nosy. Instead, Obydva asked, "What are our theories? Nat's story is more like delirium nonsense."

Vist shook their head. "It wasn't nonsense. What Nat described might seem like delirium. But then Mik and Steven also roved the west seashore of Gera. Tell him yourself, Mik. What did you see with your own eyes?"

"The svoloch," Mik said with his usual frown. "There were too many, too organised and too early for the breeding and feeding season to be so far south. They knocked Steven unconscious with a stone. I turned to go back for him and had to face the first attackers head-on. I didn't even have time to think about my zapper and walloped them with the only object in my hands – the totem. It broke in half and fell into the deep mud. However, this seemed to make an impression on the herd. They looked very frightened and fled even faster. Silently this time."

"What about the totem?" Obydva asked.

"My guys reported that they later tried to find the broken half with the help of detectors, but the damned blue salt must have been swept away by the sea. The half I still had is in the temple now with Cesario."

"I knew that Steven was injured by the svoloch, but back home you failed to mention that you were a hero again and keep saving people." Obydva smiled. "So Nat also described the strange svoloch behaviour. How odd!"

Vist nodded. "He described to Timofey how a crowd of svolochs behaved like one, looking like a giant roaring monster from a distance. It corresponds to gouged patches in the ice, a crushed wing of the station, and satellite images showing huge footprints around the station a few cycles ago. We need to walk to the hills where they came from to learn more. They must have a camp not too far."

The loader swayed, and Mik grabbed Vist's shoulder. "You should get better first. Obydva, take the architexter to the Bumblebag, and I'll check the hills."

"No, Mik, you aren't that enhanced. I have all the necessary implants. I'll go," Obydva insisted. "You must also rest and recharge your devices."

To his surprise, neither Mik nor Vist objected. Vist picked up the dark robe from the floor.

"Obydva, can I have you for a minute?" Mik dragged Obydva out of the room and slammed the door shut.

He stood still for a while, and Obydva had to ask, "What's the matter?"

"I want to show you where the second avion is. It's under the ice. Come with me, and tell me if it's possible to lift it with the power scoops on your Bumblebag."

"But what for? Do we need it now?"

"What if someone is still alive in there? Nat found the remains of only seven nordians. He stoked the stove with their gnawed bones. I don't feel anything through the ice, but you did say that I don't have enough implants."

They reached the place where the *Wasp* and the second avion of seismologists were buried in the thick ice. Obydva sat down on the ice directly above the avion and closed his eyes.

"If anyone was alive there, they are no longer. But I'm not sure. Something is interfering with the signals. It's like trying to make out written words through a window while rain hits the glass."

"That's what Vist said, something similar anyway. There was hardly any connection with the satellites through the ice. But are they there?"

"What?" Obydva looked at Mik.

"The words. Well, is there heat, a pulse or movement on board?"

Obydva touched his amulet behind his ear.

"No. And the temperature is the same throughout. If they didn't suffocate there, they froze. Unlike Nat, they couldn't build a stove."

They stood in silence for a while.

"These nordians would have a lot of relatives in Altyn District and in the mines of the foothills. One consolation will be that the svoloch didn't devour the poor shorties like those seven who Nat cremated."

"Mik, we'll go back for the *Wasp* and raise that avion too. You better explain to me what's up with you and Vist? Had a fight? I can tell I inherited female intuition from Marta and—"

"Leave it. Nothing to worry about."

And Obydva left it.

They wandered back, and Vist was already walking towards them in their robe, with a rather weak gait but ready to leave.

Vist took Obydva's hand to tell and show him what he would be looking for, but there was a peculiar lack of transparency in this connection. This was very unusual for Vist ever since the second loader had been created, but Obydva felt a sense of déjà vu that took him back to the distant past. As a loader-hybrid, he couldn't tell whose memory it was, but for a split second, Vist was again the mysterious person nobody knew anything about.

In under five minutes, Mik and Vist were on their way to the Bumblebag on a luge, and Obydva was walking towards the snowy hills. His boots had a wide force field under the soles. This spread his weight, prevented him from sinking into the snow, and accelerated his progress like skis.

He carefully watched out for the footprints, but over the many hours, the drifting snow erased them. The huge dents could still be seen if he looked carefully, but they disappeared closer to the hills, and the barely visible furrows in the snow indicated that there had recently been heavy traffic there. The dents pointed north.

Obydva followed this trail until it also became levelled by the wind. He walked for about an hour without any change in the general landscape. From the top of the first hill, he glanced back at the station once, and even with intense focus, he saw only the vague outlines of a dead settlement. It was hard to believe that quite recently this place looked like a Christmas fair in which lights had always burned brightly, and the radio sang through a satellite channel. Usually, the drum orchestras of Altyn-Grom. Obydva sighed and moved on.

Vist assured him that he wouldn't have to travel all the way to the crater, the svolochs' southernmost major dwelling. O'Teka had long known its coordinates and status. It would still be a few cycles walk from here. Could it be that the entire crowd described by Nat had gone in exactly that direction? And if not gone, then where did they find shelter here?

Obydva sensed what he was searching for long before he saw it. It started with a slight vibration under his feet, then in the air. A hum that became louder with every step. And then he found a cave.

This hole in the snow couldn't be the entrance. So it could have multiple mouths. It was an ice cave, which is quite typical for these parts. Vist wrote in his offering that a few years ago, he and Nat couldn't understand at first how the svoloch

migrated to the warm regions of Gera for childbirth
and didn't freeze on the way. After all, this path,
although warmer, is much longer than the one they
make on their pilgrimage between two homes. Also,
pregnant svolochs are less frost-resistant. Later Nat
found these caves, but Obydva didn't imagine them
to be so vast.

The ice in these parts of the permafrost was
hundreds of metres thick and as porous as sponge. It
had tunnels and quite extensive hollows. Obydva
scanned the dimensions and determined that this
cave was no smaller than the capital's ball games
arena. The thickness of its ceiling assuaged fears of a
future collapse, and the loader decided to observe
what was happening in the cave.

And   something   extraordinary   was
happening. Right in the centre, despite the losses
during the last attack on the station, a huge crowd
of svolochs sat in a large dense circle. Hundreds
were huddling there. Possibly the entire remaining
population of the crater dwellers.

Obydva knew the wild men could see well in
the darkness, but he had to switch his eyes to dark
vision. He zoomed in and decided that, after all, not
all of the population, but only an adult part of it
were there. In the centre was an empty area a few
metres in diameter in which a dark object covered
by a grassy blanket stood. The object was several

centimetres high, but the width under the blanket was undetectable. The creatures themselves also behaved strangely. They sat and howled, either from grief or from other strong emotions. Sometimes individuals jumped up and shouted out words in their meagre vocabulary. They waved their arms and struck their chests. Obydva heard the terms "mbroj" and "libertah" distinctly once or twice, but the hands of the comrades sitting beside such persons pulled them down, then forced them to sit still and compose themselves.

It looked like a rather monotonous and mind-numbing long event. Obydva settled himself comfortably on the edge of the hole, took off his shoulder bag, and set up a small insulated tent, which immediately warmed up inside. He lay down in it, took his round camera out of his eye socket, and lowered it into the hole on a long cord. Then he sealed himself inside the tent and dozed off. Later he would send everything the camera recorded via satellite to Timofey.

A noise interrupted Obydva's rest, unlike the previous repetitious rumble. He climbed out of the tent, pulled the eyeball up, and fixed it back in its place.

He looked into the cave and saw disorder. The herd howled in horror and covered their faces with their hands. All recoiled from what was happening in the centre of the ring. And in the centre, one male svoloch stood over a torn blanket and hit the mysterious object with a piece of iron pipe. Shards flew in all directions, and he repeatedly shouted the single word "ganda" in a frenzy. Soon he stopped and froze, breathing heavily. One by one, the others also fell silent and began to get up, muttering like the audience in the theatre when the performance was over and everyone had to go home. They were all moving in the same direction, carefully avoiding the creature in the middle like a stream, and then disappearing into the cave's northern tunnel. Left alone, the hairy troublemaker examined the iron in his hand, shook it victoriously over his head, and looked up. He probably saw Obydva's head in the hole in the ceiling with his nocturnal eyes because he gasped and sprinted away, following his tribe mates.

Obydva closed his eyes and listened. The vibration in the ice indicated that the tribe was steadily moving north.

The loader decided not to look for an alternative way in. He could have passed it on his way here some distance back. He produced his climbing equipment from the bag. With a slight buzz, he descended into the cave like a spider on a silver thread and approached the discarded grass blanket; there were scattered pieces of blue salt with fragments of some electronic device sticking out of them. Obydva carefully collected each piece, left the cave, and hurried back to his Bumblebag.

26. Grass Village

A young man named Paul from the Tall Grass Village went out on a mission for his headman. It was an important and secret mission. The headman himself didn't seem to understand exactly what Paul was supposed to do. But the old rogue's eyes shone with delight when he accompanied Paul to the forest's edge. Paul was sure that this task had something to do with the visit from a strangely dressed woman whom the headman was clearly afraid of more than of death itself. But after she left, the headman was very happy – he called Paul and examined him from head to toe. Then he asked if the lazy, gluttonous Paul wanted to earn favours. If he were to succeed, the headman would give him a cart to keep. Paul could collect firewood with it and make a good living.

Paul agreed. How couldn't he? His status in the village would immediately become high enough to invite the widow of the late woodcutter round to his place and even persuade her to live with him in the same hut.

Paul asked what to do. Nothing difficult was the answer. He just needed to take this heavy bundle of blue salt crystals, tightly wrapped and secured with leather belts, and carry it to the river bank in the forest. There, he had to sit down and wait for the person who would come for the crystal, get a bag with a fee from him and return.

"Just be careful. Piranha orchids have blossomed again in these parts. Don't stand too long under the trees," his leader said, smiling encouragingly.

Paul stepped into the woods without thinking.

Now on his way, however, Paul scolded himself for his frivolity. It was at least two hours walk to the river, and this is when the very first svolochs should appear in these forests, migrating from the north for "nesting." Paul felt he might regret his rushed decision.

The more Paul thought about it, the slower his pace became, and the more he wanted to return.

Finally, he became utterly scared. The river was only a few steps away. He could already hear the splashing of water on the rocks. He figured it was close enough to the bank, and he could put this bundle in the open area of dry clay under the tree. However, as soon as he released the bundle from his hands, it buzzed softly and lit up from the inside with a dim light.

It was strange, but Paul was not thinking about anything at that moment. He froze, slowly straightened up, and looked at his hands as if he had never seen them before. Then he looked around and chuckled. His face pulled an expression that none of his friends would now recognise. Not even the young daughter of the soup maker who was secretly in love with him.

Paul didn't go back. On the contrary, he went straight to the river, sat on the bank, took off his shoes, and lowered his feet in the water. So he sat there and waited for a long time.

He didn't know that a naked and very hairy man with long hair on his head and all over his back approached the water downstream. He scooped up water with his hand and began to drink, but then he sniffed his fingers attentively and noisily. Then he lifted his head and began to inhale warm air through his nostrils. A woman moaned from the thickets, and a small voice called out. "Snab?"

"Shh," the man replied, hissing. He scooped up water with both hands and carried it into the thicket. He got just a few drops to an almost equally hairy woman, who lay exhausted on a blanket made of grass. He poured water into her open mouth, pointed towards the river, and said, "Mya-so ... warten."

She smiled at him and lowered her head to the ground.

Then the man silently but quickly disappeared into the tall grass, but he somehow managed to find his way in it without it shaking or rustling. He saw a rather well-fed man sitting on the shore among the grassy tussocks, and the long shiny hair on his shoulders stood on end, so he looked like a tussock overgrown with grass. Convinced that the man was alone, he crept up behind him and froze. The man also stopped dangling his legs in the water and slowly turned his head. Their eyes met, but the naked hairy man at that moment seemed to go blind. And the well-fed man swayed, turned pale, and opened his mouth to scream.

The svoloch squeezed his throat with strong hands and said distinctly, and not at all in a simple svoloch's language, "But you don't have to do this."

Paul died quickly.

***

The svoloch was in no hurry to drag the prey to his woman. He examined his ankles and found, with satisfaction, a dry and sharp bone tied to his leg. Quickly wielding it, he bled the poor fellow and drank his hot blood for a long time, groaning and smacking his lips with pleasure. Then he gobbled up a decent chunk of Paul's liver and, belching satiated, fell on his side.

He lay like that for no longer than a minute. He woke up when a burgundy flower fell next to his face, a few centimetres from his nose. Surrounded by asymmetrical petals, its tiny mouth convulsed, with white-bluish sharp teeth snapping. The man jumped in horror and looked around in surprise at the work of his hands, listened with concern, and heaved the bloodied corpse over his neck without difficulty. And on time. In the very place where he had just been lying, a whole rain of small orchids fell, attached to stems as thin as a hair, several metres long. They fumbled and bared their teeth as if in frustration. Not finding any prey, they pulled back into the tree's dense, almost black crown one by one.

The man returned a few minutes later and scraped the ground with his nails for a long time until he mixed the rest of the blood with the mud. He splashed river water on the bank and kicked dirt into the river with his feet. When there was no smell of blood on the damp ground, he calmed down and hurried back to his mate.

And the quiet, extinguished bunch of translucent bluish crystals had disappeared by the end of the next cycle. Who took it from the deserted riverbank? No one knew.

27. Bumblebag

Mik picked the bluish shard up and looked through it at the light.

"This totem is a lot like the one I broke. Only, this one was not a mantelpiece ornament but was simply walled up in crystals and pulled together with a rubber strap. At least, that's how Obydva's eye saw it before the destruction. And the device inside is again hopelessly damaged."

Vist was much more interested in the device's wreckage.

"And yet it is very similar to a simple device for communication or broadcasting ... not a radio, no. But it definitely received and transmitted waves. Cesario will figure it out in no time."

"But why salt? And why blue? Copper sulphate?"

"The blue salt is a mixture and contains it too, but copper sulphate is bright blue. This is darker and has a dirty green tint. It includes a lot of other mineral impurities, including organic ones and plenty of mica. Understanding how it blocks our detectors but allows this device to do its job will be very interesting."

Vist scrutinised a piece of the gadget intently, like an entomologist with an unusual bug in his hand, and with a curious, appreciative smile. Thick long hair on the right side of their head drooped over Vist's shoulder like a scarf.

Mik snatched the item from the loader's hand and dropped it on the table. Then he took Vist by the elbows and firmly turned to face him. He decided this was a good time to talk. Waiting until they were alone again would be a painful choice. Nat was still asleep, and Obydva's sensors worked outwards while he was flying the Bumblebag. Instead of eavesdropping, his friend's ears monitored the vessel's air pressure and listened to his favourite music until they landed.

Mik peered into Vist's face, hoping to see what he needed so much now and had needed for a long time. Green eyes looked at him with warmth and some affection. The face lacked a gentle blush, and the smile lacked invitation. But Mik tried to remember it was a waste of time to expect any common emotions from Vist.

"What did you want to tell me, Mik?" a steady voice said.

"To tell you? Shouldn't we talk about what happened at that station?"

"Is something left unclear? In my opinion, everything went very nicely and beautifully. It seemed to me that you felt good."

"Very good. But what does that mean? I might be a loader too now, but not at your level. I still feel like a man of Earth. What now?"

Vist raised one eyebrow in genuine surprise. "What now? Now you know my secret, and if I had the slightest thought that you would betray it to anyone, this would not have happened."

"Of course, but that's not what I'm talking about." Mik felt very awkward but continued. "I know my reasons ... at least now. In that moment, I could not think at all. But you, Vist; why did you—"

Vist stepped towards Mik, took his cold hand with warm fingers, and suddenly pressed it to their cheek. Vist's face also felt warm.

"You saved my life. It would be strange if I failed to fill with gratitude and other appropriate feelings. We were both glad. We were celebrating life, reunion and love."

Mik wasn't just surprised. He was shocked, but his lips stretched into a happy smile. He closed his eyes and almost whispered, "I could never imagine that Vist was capable of even considering love. Does Vist love me? It's unimaginable."

"Of course I do. You have everything that I can and should love."

Mik stopped smiling and opened his eyes, "Can you hear yourself? There is metal in your voice. You can say in the same tone that you love Steve, Zina or Rod!"

"I do love them. Not romantically, but they, like you, deserve love."

"And if one of them rescued you from the ice, you would ...?"

Vist let go of Mik's hand and laughed. "You mean, if one of them became my hero and saved the

241

most precious thing I have? And they would have the same reasons for doing so? Mik, what do you think? Tell me, where does true love begin? True romance? There are many people in the world you can fall in love with, but for some reason, this happens only with the person you must first meet on your journey. Second, this person has to possess the traits and values you seek. Third, this person must consistently and naturally prove their integrity, which grants you precious and absolute trust, respect and adoration. You find that you belong together, like individuals of the same "species" or type of mind. You enjoy each other's company, and at the right romantic moment, voilà! All conditions add up to the only possible result. Love is a conditional thing, and romantic love is very conditional. Conditions are necessary, Mik. For true love to be born, live and change – to grow with us. It happened to us at that station, and we celebrated. It wasn't the beginning of something to ask, 'Now what?' It was a natural phase in a complex process that started years ago, long before you and I sensed something different towards each other. The next stage will depend on our choices and on the conditions. Both of these are quite important."

Vist kissed Mik affectionately on the lips and laughed so casually and cheerfully that Mik felt better, as if the chain that bound him loosened, and he could breathe again.

Vist was right. This is exactly how the whole thing happened, and those words described the exact course of events, although Mik never thought to apply them to Vist before. Now he wanted to grab and squeeze Vist in a bear hug. He wanted to taste those delicious lips again and smell honey wax in the mass of chestnut hair, but he stopped himself with a mighty effort. There will be a better time when the risk of compromising Vist's secret would be minimal. Conditions, huh? He would take care of at least some of them.

Mik and Vist went back to packing the pieces of blue salt found by Obydva in the ice cave, and the occasional touch of the elbows or eye contact filled Mik with indescribable happiness. He was twenty years old again and felt like there was a real earthly April outside the ship walls. He imagined his favourite room in his house, with the flame in the log burner, looking almost scarlet when viewed through a glass of wine. A mass of quilts on the floor and a huge platter of cheese and smoked sandies. Only now, Vist was there too.

The voice of Obydva destroyed this mirage in one second.

"Guys, we've got a problem. I lost contact with my controls. Everyone, go to the evacuation cabin immediately. I'll meet you there, and don't forget Nat. I woke him up from here already."

Mik, without further ado, rushed to the passenger section, where Nat, automatically awakened by his own bed, should be coming round. Mik barely noticed Vist snatch a piece of the device from the totem, tuck it into the folds of their robes, close their eyes, and freeze, both hands resting on the cargo-bay wall. Vist always knows what to do, Mik thought, pushing away an unfamiliar urge to prioritise the architexter, and not at all because of Vist's important title.

Nat was already on his feet and even dressed, but he looked confused. He was just beginning to understand the situation.

"Hurry up, buddy," Mik had to call out as the craft tilted terribly. The engine's steady rumble gave way to a hysterical squeal – a mixture of the falling avion and an alarm.

Mik took two emergency backpacks off the wall and tossed one to Nat.

"We're falling," Nat mumbled, putting the backpack on.

"Let's go," Mik replied. He grabbed Nat by the chest strap and dragged him into the avion's tail. They had to run up the tilted passage, but not far. Obydva was already in the evacuation cabin.

"Where's Vist?" shouted Mik as he fastened the staggering Nat to a recess with softened walls.

Obydva listened in. "Coming. But I don't see how that's possible ... he's not alone. Who, how and where?"

Vist appeared at the hatch with a large sack over their shoulders. It was not clear what it was made of. As soon as the first loader was inside, Obydva waved his hand, sealed the escape cabin, and shouted, "Here goes nothing!"

Seconds later the Bumblebag entered the ocean.

28. Davon Marchel

Message to His Wisdom or anyone in the temple who can read this language.

My name is Davon Marchel. My regiment selected me to spy in the Salty Village for four months while the replacement for the deceased Savana Brone was altered and trained. I was the best qualified because of my appearance and skills. I wasn't too happy about it, but I knew it was a short assignment, followed by a safe departure.

But things didn't work out well, not at all.

I know I won't escape this trap I have fallen into myself. I want to do the only one thing available to me in my situation. A confession! I committed a terrible sin, and I am paying for it. Unfortunately, along with me, innocent victims also suffered. And this is another burden on my conscience. But only O'Teka knows the depth of my remorse.

About a year before my post in the Salty Village as a spy, I became too interested in the technology of loaders, namely neural-loading. I prayed to everything on the subject available at my level in the temple. I was even an apprentice to one of the surgeons in New Tokyo to gain access to his offerings, which were restricted to mere physicians. I began to have interesting ideas about not just obtaining information from a person's consciousness but also introducing someone else's perception into the human mind. However, everything remained at the level of ideas when I took up my post outside the colony and away from the temple. Upon my return, I intended to continue my studies, and I even suggested proposing a project to the architexter. Most likely, His Wisdom would see more harm than good in it. I was even more than sure of this after what my ideas did a few cycles ago.

As a spy I failed. The Great Martyr, Morbus Contagione, exposed me after the first two weeks. I botched my mission. I don't want to talk about how it happened. I am ashamed that I was weak and never believed in what this creature was capable of. I can only say that my fear for the integrity of my flesh turned out to be stronger than my will to remain loyal to the colony. I betrayed the colony. I confess that I told this tech-hungry and control-craving monster about my ideas to save my skin. It was all I had, valuable enough to buy my life, and all I could offer for my chance to escape the nightmare. How short-sighted I was!

Morbus left me alone for almost half a month, but she removed my communicator from my ear and, every three cycles, with a knife at my throat, she made sure I sent a routine signal to the colony to say that I was all right. I obediently followed this ritual, and my fear only grew as my first wounds healed.

Finally, she came to me and asked me what materials I needed to build a device that would allow her to manipulate the minds of the wild ones. I told her. Initially, Morbus said that svoloch had inherited respect for incomprehensible technology and wanted me to create something to control them and make them safe. But then this project turned into something much worse. For many weeks, I lived under the floor at Morbus's house. They fed me well and brought me large black leaves and phosphorus ink. Then Morbus began to bring medical devices and some equipment I requested, the origin of which was obvious.

The first device I built, a prototype, was useless to Morbus, but I unexpectedly got so excited about what it could do that my desire to succeed overwhelmed me. I felt I was working on an offering to the temple archives, and my work would become a brick in the walls of the great temple. So what kept me going? Thoughts that I remain faithful to O'Teka because knowledge remains above all for me, and I create this knowledge despite the conditions. I called my creation a decognitivator because it violates the person's mind, depriving him of forming his own opinion, of making a decision or of being accountable for his actions.

Whether insane or desperate, I improved a cursed device and then tested it on my tormentor. However, Morbus turned out to be too educated and smart, so much so that my decognitivator didn't work on her. It didn't affect me, nor the mind of another villager out of all those unwittingly brought to Morbus's house for a test. But it worked. It easily penetrated the minds of young and older people and of those adults who spent most of their lives here. For recent exiles still capable of critical thinking, the device didn't work, although it gave them and me the most horrid headaches.

Finally, Morbus stated that if people from the colony, who were affected by the device, went into exile, they must be in the capital itself. It looked like she had already chosen her victim. That Morbus had an accomplice in the colony, I no longer doubted. I panicked. I said that the decognitivator must not cross borders. The temple detectors and satellite scanners would quickly discover the electronic device with its strong electromagnetic output. The loaders may become interested in unfamiliar signals, if not during the experiment, then soon after. And the signal would be tracked all the way here.

I'm not sure, but I think that when I mentioned the loaders, an incredibly vicious expression appeared on the martyr's already unpleasant face. Morbus left with both devices I'd made, and I didn't see her for several cycles. Guards brought water and food and changed the bucket but didn't answer questions. My betrayal of everything sacred to me was now undeniable. Morbus planned to use this model to access the information I lacked. I told her about its location myself in fear of torment.

When Morbus returned, she showed me my device, lined and bound with bluish cloudy crystals, and said that she had made a trip to the north to test the device on a stupid and easy svoloch. She stole the whole avion for that trip, but only for a day, as she could not handle it alone. I was horrified. How the decognitivator acted on the wild ones, I can't even imagine. Morbus didn't let me in on the details, saying only that thanks to these crystals, the colonists couldn't even find a spaceship in some distant crater, let alone a small device. I realised that now my creation had reached the colony.

I heard about the fire in the city by chance from two guards who changed at the post. One of them was almost deaf in both ears. And so the second one yelled so hard that even I could hear him in the basement. This wasn't the first time I had learned of the major events in the village in this manner. Later, I told Morbus I would not help her any more, but she again took up the knife and ... oh! I don't remember how I ended up on the filthy floor of my prison, where I burst into tears. In my fear, I became the victim of my own experiment. And next to me lay Morbus, looking very pleased with herself. She was naked. I didn't immediately notice that I was also partially undressed, and I couldn't even imagine how long I was out of my mind under the influence of my own device. My upper arms were scratched to blood, and I saw skin under my nails, but I didn't remember doing it.

The damned witch had her way with me. And with my own hands, I constructed a means of physical violence for her, in which she violates both the body and the mind. She finally took over my whole being and bent it to do her dirty will.

I unquestioningly obeyed her again, this time motivated only by her promise not to repeat with me the most unthinkable act that I had to undergo. I made a more advanced third device, but I never learned about the results of other experiments. Morbus looked satisfied, but her demands grew. She demanded the creation of a another one that would work both ways. She wanted not only to control a person but also to gain access to their senses and experience their sensations – especially taste. I obeyed but decided it was time to end this. If she wanted to fuck herself, literally, then let her do it without using my flesh. But what can I do? Just end this life and hope that, at least in this way, I will minimise the evil I unleashed into this world.

I was lucky. A young village woman whose curious mind had led her into the house during a service agreed to help me. I don't know whether she managed to get to the border gate and convince the guards. But she brought me this very scalpel with which I'm recording my story. Morbus no longer descends into my cell. I really hope that these inscriptions will be seen not by her but by someone else. Someone who will carry my testimony to His Wisdom, Vist the architexter.

I will wait until the last moment, but if Morbus brings me new material to make more decognitivators, it will force me to do the only thing in my power.

Oh no! Now the witch just has started to skin someone right above my head. It's unbearable to listen.

Forgive me, people of Gera. I am sorry, my master.

My last thoughts will be with you, my beloved Lark Grayson.

Time to go.

D.M.

29. Grotovaya

The parachuted emergency escape cabin reached the water after the waves above the good old Bumblebag calmed down, and the vortex disappeared. Using the built-in satellite navigation, it automatically oriented itself and started moving towards the nearest coast. But the passengers in it were not only conscious but also very agitated. Even Nat was totally alert by now and was the first to speak up.

"What's this?" he said, nodding at the motionless bundle in the middle of the cabin.

Now he could see this bundle was a bent human body wrapped in a blanket of black grass and twigs.

"The reason for our downfall, I suppose," Obydva said and looked at Vist. "Why didn't any of us hear it? Why didn't I feel it?"

He raised his hand, and the capsule's luminous ceiling became much brighter.

"Are you okay?" asked Mik, turning to Vist.

"Yes, thank you," replied Vist, reaching for the blanket and unravelling it.

Everyone saw a figure curled up into a ball. Its back, neck and head were covered with shiny long hair. The creature was immobilised, but the frightened dark eye under the shaggy fringe sparkled furiously. Vist's metallic words sounded. "Unfortunately, we weren't paying enough attention. But don't judge yourself harshly. One of the ways the svoloch so successfully masked the number of individuals in their groups was through their ability to synchronise their heartbeats. This time the smart saboteur blended with us. That's why we didn't hear the one extra pulse. Only during the fall did everyone's pulse quicken, but not this one, so I soon found her."

"Her?" Nat stared at the svoloch with surprise.

"Yes," Obydva said, "she isn't as hairy as the males."

"She also has a blanket," Vist said, "Nat, you were the first to report from the crater that only females make blankets. I never had a chance to study one."

Nat frowned, wondering why Vist was examining the blanket so closely. "What's with it?"

"Why haven't you ever brought me an exhibit like this from your expedition?"

"Vist, why would I? Did you expect me to steal it from one of the women?"

"Look!" Vist took the edge of the blanket and stretched it out with their fingers. Small crystals of blue salt sparkled in the light of the luminous ceiling, like tiny beads between strong blades of grass and thin twigs. "This sand is crystals of blue salt stuck to the grass. It can't be glue, it's more like the resin of some plants or algae."

Nat shrugged. "I haven't seen it before."

"Because you never had a chance to look at it so closely. Our captives in the past were all males. But someone somehow learned about the jamming properties of this mineral, and perhaps it was from these blankets. Who studied the svoloch of Noverca better than Nat?"

Vist looked around at their comrades. It was evident from their faces that they were all thinking about the same person; therefore, there was no need to mention his name.

Vist carried on, "Now you can explain the final mystery of their ability to remain undetected by our scanners in your next essay. Simple mica would not be enough. It's a special property of blue salt we need to study."

"True, but how did she manage to bring down the whole avion?"

"The same way she or her friend brought down the transport with my imports," Obydva said.

Vist nodded. "Yes, only this time she somehow knew exactly which cables to bite through."

"Experienced, hah?" Nat turned to Obydva, "I am so sorry for your loss. Bumblebag was the best. I will miss her too."

"I won't," Obydva replied. "I don't have attachments to inanimate objects any more. It was a good machine, but it's time for an upgrade. You better worry about the *Wasp*. How do we cut it out of the ice without my ray drill?"

Then, Nat really started to wonder what life would be like for him if he didn't get the *Wasp* back.

Mik was still watching the svoloch on the floor. "I am concerned by the recent number of cases in which these creatures are involved and acting out of character. Vist, surely you have some idea by now."

Vist touched the amulet above his or her ear and shifted closer to the creature. The svoloch's invisible binds had loosened enough for her to move her head. Now Nat could see two frightened eyes.

"Klicha, Vist," the loader said as they touched their head and then pointed to the svoloch's forehead. "Klicha?"

After the creature studied the loader for a long minute, she finally said her name in a broken voice. "Astuta."

"Astuta? Dob." Vist took the piece of smashed totem from their pocket and showed it to Astuta. "Shta evo?"

The dark eyes opened wide and rolled in horror. Astuta squealed and shook her head furiously, unable to move her limbs.

Vist hid the piece in their robe, waited for the svoloch to get tired, and then asked again. "Shta?"

Astuta finally replied, "Ganda! Hullu! Ganda! Ganda!"

"Ganda?" Vist looked back at Nat. "This word wasn't used by them before. Have you heard it?"

Nat shook his head then shrugged.

Obydva said, "I heard that word yesterday, in an ice cave full of svoloch. Do you two really know their lingo?"

"Perhaps now you can call it that, although it consists of a few words borrowed from several Earth languages," Nat said. "Mostly, these are words from Ancient Eurasia. I don't know the word 'Ganda,' though."

"It means beauty in Filipino, but it doesn't fit here in context," Mik said.

"Well, I don't know." Vist peered at the scarred and pale-skinned face. "Blue salt is abundant in northern ice-land. These people found it and appreciated the beauty of translucent crystals so much that they embroidered their blankets with the smallest ones. They couldn't have known right away that it was also camouflage. Then the salt became a casing for the device that now frightens Astuta, but the name was not changed. By the way, 'hullu' means 'crazy' in Finnish."

"So what are you going to do with this ... Astuta?" Mik asked. "Even a small svoloch individual could be a hazard to bring to the colony."

"It will be risk-free in my house," Vist answered. "I could try and work on something I always wanted, but I felt reluctant to take another svoloch prisoner for my study. After all, they are people, not animals to take samples from. Astuta came to us, ruined the avion, and now she is our prisoner. It's a good opportunity to learn more about blue salt and svolochs too. She might help shed some light on certain mysteries, and then I'll take her back to the crater."

As Vist spoke, Astuta listening intently, clearly reacting to mentions of her own name. Finally, she growled reproachfully, and Nat translated. "Many ... words. Fog."

And then the bottom of the cabin rustled in the gravel of shallow water, and it stopped. You could hear the surf splashing against the walls outside. They arrived at the shore. Obydva opened the hatch, and Mik got out first with a prisoner on his shoulder, followed by Vist and Nat. Obydva programmed the vessel for an automatic return to the port of Pettogreko and joined his comrades, knee-deep in water, as they plodded towards the high dry land. Behind them, the emptied cabin folded into a streamlined shape and disappeared into the waves.

Mik asked, "If you can program any course, why did you fly your avion yourself?"

"Because I love it," replied Obydva without expression.

"Couldn't we go all the way home in that capsule?"

"No. This capsule must go around the mainland from the south to get to the west coast. We will not survive such a long and hot journey, so it will be easier and faster to cross it by land. Good thing Gera is not as broad as long, and we better call out a pickup."

"Do you feel how warm it is here? The temperate southern zone," said Nat, discovering that they had no connection with the colony here, "The satellite makes it appear that we are indeed on the east side of Gera."

"On our way down, we deviated greatly from the course." Obydva pointed to the south and added, "In that direction, there should be a village of outcasts called Grotovaya. They live in grottoes."

"Okay, I'll ask Timofey to send us a conmot," said Mik and produced his amulet.

In the meantime, Nat loosened Astuta's binds, stood her up to her feet, and threw a grassy blanket over her shoulders like a cloak. Now only the arms of the captive were immobilised. She was still scared, but she dutifully walked along the shore with the others, trying to stay close to Nat. Perhaps his long white hair or ability to understand her inspired her confidence somewhat.

They reached the village after several hours of walking. For the loaders, this was nothing, but Astuta also looked like she was no stranger to long walks.

There was only one street in the village – a long and sheer bank of high rocky sediments, with one clear line indicating the level the water reached at high tide. From the flat sandy beach, simple flights of stairs rose up to it, and above that line, Nat could see rows of entrances to grottoes. To an Earthman, who grew up among fishermen and hunters on the river, they reminded him of the long-forgotten nests of sand swallows. Nat thought that a long time ago, the water used to rise higher and create these caves.

Before entering Grotovaya, they stopped for a bite to eat, pulling food from their backpacks. They offered Astuta their dry rations, but she sniffed them once and refused.

"Svolochs don't cook their food. It has to be raw, even if it's not too fresh," Nat said. "Maybe for her, we can trade something uncooked in the village?"

But in Grotovaya, apparently, it was the sleeping hours, and only one guard sat at the stone pier. He didn't immediately notice the travellers, as he sat with his back to them and admired the yellow clouds over Vitr. He was rather young and had violet skin without scales; he had a muscular build and wore old knee-length trousers.

He was surprised to see the travellers, but at the sight of the svoloch, he could not even scream and was about to sprint away, but Mik caught him and held him until he calmed down and listened. After a small outburst of panic and worry, the exile finally pulled himself together and heard Nat's request. Looking sideways at the caves, he said, "I have nothing to offer you. When the fishermen wake up, maybe then."

But the young man couldn't resist when Obydva produced a package of oatmeal biscuits from his bag.

"Okay, I'll get you some fish myself."

Grumbling non-stop that all sorts of people are lurking around and walking their domesticated svolochs without collars, he trotted to several large barrels of water that stood by one of the stairs. The young man opened one of them and dragged a hairless pale creature with three round black eyes and a birdlike beak out of it on a rope. It was about the size of a small dog but too skinny and limp to be a blobster. But that was precisely what it was.

In shock, Nat and his comrades watched as the young man dragged the obviously starved blobster to the sea, swung it on a rope, and threw it into the green waves. He didn't release the rope's end but unwound it several metres, allowing the animal to swim away. When the water began to boil in one place, he pulled the animal to the beach and threw it on the sand. No more than two minutes passed. The hungry blobster stuffed his stomach or goitre to capacity. Through the stretched translucent skin, sea dwellers and some small fish were visible, still moving. However, the blobsters' organism could not take this extreme. The whitish body thrashed and twitched, and the blobster lying on its back vomited. Now the haul was splashing and beating their tails on the sand – wet with water and blood.

The young man looked rather proud, if not smug. Astuta squealed with joy and, falling to her knees, grabbed the fish with her teeth and started working with her jaws.

But Nat threw up his hands and shouted at the young man. "And you call this fishing? Are you completely wild here? Immediately untie and release the animal into the sea!"

The young man looked surprised and recoiled, saying, "There is no point in this. It has already been used up."

Nat didn't understand and looked back at the blobster. Vist was squatting beside it. The animal still lay on its back, with its head rising off the ground. Its beak was wide open, and its round black eyes stared in amazement. Blobsters don't have eyelids, so those eyes never closed when the semi-gills stopped fluttering under its beak.

"It's dead," Vist said, and Mik turned abruptly and headed for the rest of the barrels. Obydva followed him.

With his foot, Mik knocked them all over, poured water onto the ground, and found two more half-dead blobsters with ropes around their necks. He cut them free and took one in his arms, and Obydva took the other. They brought animals to the fish on the sand and carefully let them eat one at a time. Meanwhile, Nat shook the villager, flashed angrily, and shouted, "I'll tear your village to hell if I find out about at least one more such fishing. Where did you get blobsters? How could you catch them yourself? You have no boats, only rafts!"

Vist put their hand on Nat's shoulder and said, "Stop it. Let me."

Nat let go of the villager, who only gritted his teeth harder and blinked fast. Vist's same hand moved from Nat's shoulder to the villager's forehead. After half a minute, the loader removed his hand and said to Nat, "I'm done here. We've got to go. Our transport must be on its way."

Several villagers woke up from the noise, and their heads appeared in the holes in the caves. However, none came down, but the released young exile nimbly climbed up the stairs and disappeared into one of the grottoes.

Vist had to wait until Obydva and Mik were confident that the two surviving blobsters had digested a small portion and would not glut themselves to death when released into the sea.

The group had to find a path to the top of the coastal ridge without the help of the villagers, and after a couple of hours of waiting, they heard the noise of an approaching truck driven by one of the ordermen. The svoloch at first refused to board the conmot until Nat covered her head with a blanket of grass and said, "Astuta, nay mbroj. Nero."

After the Grotovaya village experience, everyone's mood was even worse than after the loss of the avion. The expression of disbelief in the blobster's bottomless eyes still lingered in everyone's mind. Nat knew that none of them would forget it soon enough. On the way to the colony's eastern gates, Mik asked Vist, "What did you find out from the exiled boy?"

"I don't have much," Vist replied thoughtfully. "It isn't clear who caught and delivered the animals to the village. The young villager just saw that it was a woman, and she brought them on a dinghy small enough to cross the continent via the river. He was more interested in her boat than her face. The woman traded live blobsters for a crop of dream pears. All I can say is that the appearance of the dinghy suspiciously matches the description given to Steven by his graduate Mirovska."

30. Cesario

Elya dutifully trudged behind Mrs Alloway and wondered into which of the most terrible abysses his life would now fall. Although Vist said he was not in trouble, his situation wasn't so simple. He didn't want to harm anyone, but Elya had brought a potentially dangerous thing to the temple, and now he felt very uneasy. To be invited to a meeting in one of the temple halls, where not only the architexter but also the Grand of the colony was going to be, didn't bode well for Elya.

Master Andrea Alloway looked back at him, "Come on, chop-chop!" She opened the self-sliding door with a wave of her hand.

Elya had never been in this hall. Or even on this floor. Here stood the famous round table, made by the architexter from the polished half of the meteorite. It is said that the second such iron table, from the other half, stands in the architexter's mansion. In the centre of the table, the holographic projector was turned off, but next to Vist's empty chair stood his assistant with the holographic face of an old man with a very stylish moustache, waiting. This was the first time Elya didn't recognise Cesario's chosen face. At the table sat several familiar and unfamiliar people in various uniforms. Grand, a man with high cheekbones, shiny, thick scales and broad shoulders characteristic of uzhans, was sitting to the left of the architexter's chair, discussing something with his secretary.

Mrs Alloway sat down next to her husband and pointed to one of the chairs at the table for Elya, next to General King. Now Elya was totally terrified, but he obediently sat down and heard Master McLeod talking to Dr Darkwood.

"At first, I didn't believe Mik, but Vist made her robe herself, so it may well have mechanisms that scouts can only dream of. Zina, can you imagine how quickly we would have taken over all of Noverca if we had all been equipped with that?"

Dr Darkwood replied, "If we all were loaders of that level? Is that what you mean? No? I can imagine, but that's what the bio-suit is for, to work together with the organism. We don't know all of its potential. Maybe it's a matter of time before ordinary humans can wear it."

"Yes, maybe Vist can survive not only in ice but also in outer space."

"Steven, this is too much! I doubt it."

"You said it, Zin. A matter of time."

In that moment, Vist entered the hall as if hosting a ball. He seemed in a good mood and didn't look like a judge. Elya felt a little better.

The architexter gave a handsome smile and greeted everyone, including the strangers in uniform. "Friends, you all know Cesario, especially if you are temple regulars. Recently, a series of sad and strange events took place in the colony, very dramatic and even threatening. My friends and I investigated them in the best traditions of the detective skills we inherited from Earth's culture. I am grateful to the colleagues of mine, representatives of the Grand's office, graduates of the scout academy and the ordermen for their help and actions. All the information we collected – evidence, witness statements and satellite imagery material – were transferred to my assistant, who analysed them and summarised the most reasonable conclusions. I suggest you listen carefully to him."

One man from the Grand's office asked loudly, "With respect, Master Architexter, I had the impression that this analysis would be done personally by you. Your assistant is an artificial. Are you sure that his conclusions can be trusted?"

"Just like I possess more tools than you, Mr Kadday, to work with the database, Cesario's intelligence has more than I have. But if it would ease you, we worked together. Cesario, please, let us begin."

The tall hooded figure cleared his throat and spoke softly with an accent oddly similar to Dr Darkwood's. "Mesdames et Messieurs! It would be unscientific and presumptuous of me to insist on the finality of my conclusions. I hope I just made things clearer for you to see the connections. So what do we have in front of us? A fire, an assassination attempt and the recent incident in the temple. First, there is the undeniable link between the fire and the blackmail attempt on our mechanic." Cesario turned his sharp, cunning eyes on the young man.

Everyone turned their heads, and Elya wanted to die on the spot.

"Messages were left on the wall of his house and the wall of the factory that was set on fire. In these two cases, they were done with one hand. I have studied every pixel of the images and have no doubt about it. Nevertheless, they were left by two different people."

"One hand and two people? How is that possible?" asked one of the ordermen guests, and everyone finally forgot about Elya.

"I believe I have an explanation, but please let me offer it to you later. Thank you. To save time and not confuse anyone, I will start not from the beginning but from the end, that is, from the most recent event. A young village woman appeared at the city gates and became so noisy that the guard was forced to listen to her. From her demands, it became clear that she knew something about the causes of the fire and that one of our fellow citizens was being held captive in her village. Learning the old tricks by which the villagers in the past tried to enter the city, the girl was treated with the appropriate precautions. She really had important information and was sent to her parents' farm on bail, but the next cycle she went back outside the civil borders."

"Another attempt at provocation?" asked one of the visitors.

"Indeed, this is what it looks like. In the past, after such an act, we would react accordingly to both her words and herself, but in this situation, nothing is as simple as it seems. She brought us a message from Davon Marchel, a failed spy in Salty Village." Cesario paused dramatically and looked around the audience with his hands behind his back. "As soon as the girl mentioned this name to Master McLeod, many mysterious factors fell into place. Our spy was not only discovered by the mystics in the village but also exploited. It was a big mistake to send this man as a temporary agent outside the colony, even as an urgent measure. Not only was he psychologically unprepared, but his abilities gave a hostile society a means to control the minds of vulnerable individuals. Therefore, I am convinced that the girl didn't run away again but was kidnapped. One of the victims, Scarlett Da Costa, reported to us that she once too experienced a strange loss of memories and stopped visiting the architexter's house. Now we know why. The observed behaviour of the villagers and some townspeople, including both Crossich and our young Mr Goryn, is not entirely their own."

Elya felt how tense and unpleasant the atmosphere had become in the hall. The last words were almost drowned in the excited roar of commentary, indignation and questions from the temple's visitors. Only the Law Force team sat and watched silently.

Vist stepped closer to the table and placed several pieces of a bluish crystal on the smooth surface with the remains of thin wires and parts of the device inside the largest shards. Elya noticed that the card he had brought wasn't among these pieces.

"Unfortunately, I was not in the city when the village woman testified," said the voice with a metallic undertone. "Maybe I could scan information that she couldn't tell herself coherently enough. These instruments were created by Mr Marchel, perhaps under duress. We learned about his personal goals and passions, which became our troubles. There are two interesting factors here. First, the device itself. It is quite complex, although it is made from our own disassembled equipment, which fell into the hands of the villagers through the smuggling and robbery of a seismic station. Evidently, Mr Marchel is more knowledgeable in loader-building technology than his status should allow him to be. We have yet to figure out how he gained access to this information and the schematics of my scanners. I must admit that his idea is almost brilliant but very dangerous. The second factor is a casing substance that didn't allow our scanner to detect the device during a work series. But we found the devices by tracking this blue salt, or "ganda," as the svolochs call it, which is rare in our parts. First, we found a city artist who completed several commissions and made a greeting card from blue salt and some innocent-looking ornaments. I spoke with him. He was not aware that he was helping to disguise the devices."

"Unfortunately, you found these tools damaged," Grand said.

"Unfortunately or fortunately? This is another question. We have the only intact device among our evidence, but I would not risk bringing it here. There might be vulnerable people among us who could be influenced by it."

The orderman sitting closer to Vist recoiled from the pieces on the table as if they, too, were able to influence him and said, "What are you going to do?"

"We will use this technology against the criminal to render them harmless. The witness pointed to the leader of the Salty Village. We could send a military force there, but we do not know how many such devices are in the hands of the Great Martyr. Our detectives observed the effect of the device on svolochs. They lost their survival instinct and died in huge numbers. To avoid such losses among the highly susceptible villagers, we need to send another emissary: well-protected, strong-minded and equipped to find the missing information. Hopefully, we can also rescue the kidnapped girl and Davon Marchel. Mrs Alloway, would you help us?"

Vist turned to Master Andrea, but she put her hand on Elya's shoulder and replied, "We will be happy to. This young man volunteers brilliant and dangerous ideas of his own to redeem himself. Don't you, Mr Goryn? With his invention, we don't need totems of blue salt, but you, the architexter, will be able not only to hear but also to see everything your infiltrator has to face."

She was smiling, and Elya suddenly felt happy and startled at the same time. He spent hours boring his new master with his "unique" design of amulet insertions. It looked like that time was not spent in vain after all.

31. Tilda

Matilda wasn't stupid, but she had a weakness that Morbus used and made her so susceptible to her influence. That weakness was her dream pears addiction and obsession with Steven. This time, she was driven by carefully planned revenge and turned off the ZPE engine in the dinghy long before she approached the yacht, slowly rowing with an oar. She tried to make as little noise as possible but soon heard loud music playing on board. Matilda sighed. Steven used to love listening to Rosa Jora in their romantic encounters and was now playing Ledomir Bessill, Carib's fifth concerto. It must be the playlist of the young girl with a fin on her head. Old philanderer! Tilda heard he was now hitting on the young cadet.

Jealousy and resentment boiled inside her again. So many years passed, and Matilda was still jealous of him for all the women on Gera and the islands, who were purple, hairy and scaly, and especially that doctor with the dark skin. Matilda, of course, was no longer young and pretty, but that doctor was probably twice her age. One consolation was that Steven's old passion for her remained unreciprocated.

But his date. Ah! Never mind. Morbus said she would deal with them both. Tilda just needed to bring the device close enough. Morbus promised she would do that without taking over Matilda this time.

The high northern side of the yacht hid Matilda's tiny boat. She froze when she heard laughter and movement on the deck above her head. She couldn't see what was happening there but saw two long shadows on the calm green waves almost beside her: a man and a woman. Steven and ... oh no! She recognised Dr Zina more by voice than shape.

Zina spoke up. "I didn't know you had a cat on your yacht."

"He's my assistant. He devours every leepoon that inadvertently sticks to the yacht's gear during a storm. They fly high above the waves. Because of them, the height and shape of the ship had to be altered."

Matilda had never heard such total happiness in his voice. So, they had eventually decided to be together. It looked by the shadow's shape that Steven was trying to put his arms around Dr Zina, but she was delaying him playfully. Her voice was also happy and flirty.

"What's his name? Your cat?"

"Bucephalus."

"Where is he now?"

"Still on the lower deck, in my study, I guess."

"What is he doing there?"

"I don't know. Studying?"

And then he kissed her. In that silence, Matilda gritted her teeth and heard the voice in her head. "Stop it. Your emotion is too strong. It interferes—"

"I can't help it," whispered Matilda.

"Stupid girl, you better calm down."

The kissing couple breathed heavily and soon hurried to the lower cabin, most likely to bed.

"Looks like he's getting there. I can have him in his next state, but you're standing in my way." And with these words, Morbus broke her promise and took over Matilda's body, but only for Matilda to slam her forehead against the bench of the boat and lose consciousness. Morbus was free to go elsewhere. And she did.

***

It was like climbing into someone else's house, where the owner is doing their own thing and does not yet know that their uninvited guest is carefully looking around and listening.

The main thing was that this was the body of an Earthman. Finally! Hardly touched by Vitr's ultraviolet radiation, pale and covered in scars, the body wasn't young but was incredibly strong and mobile. It rang and burned with excitement. Morbus felt a dull pain in some old wounds and joints – souvenirs of the man's past adventures, but his hand confidently and knowledgably caressed the hot female body, so soft, dark and smooth. This woman with thick braids was attractive, but it was hard to enjoy her looks because the man was shutting his eyes too much. They both breathed as if inhaling each other. Something like electrical jolts shook both of them from time to time. Morbus had met them before, but it was so long ago that it didn't matter. What they were up to was much more important.

The man wasn't doing exactly what Morbus missed so much. It was unclear why he often pressed his lips to a woman's mouth. Morbus had never needed a kiss, neither in this life nor in her previous one, when she was a man.

Nevertheless, it was good to feel the muscles in the legs and the hips tensing up again, to experience these long-forgotten sensations of rhythmic beats and the sliding of skin against skin.

A minute later, the martyr caught the woman's scent. It was different. It made Morbus dizzy with glee. The smell of some fragrant oil joined these sensations. Some unfamiliar flowers or herbs with which this woman perfumed her body, making it even more desirable and supple.

Finally, the blond-haired man, whom Tilda always stared at more than necessary, completely lost himself in this storm of delight. This was what Morbus had been waiting for. Now! When the man's strong back arched, a wild roar of the beast suddenly replaced his passionate groan.

The woman froze. Did she sense that something had changed here? Something was wrong with her lover. He stopped and tensed awkwardly, then sneered and scratched his left shoulder vigorously with his right hand, leaving red lines. A hot drop of his saliva fell on her cheek. She struggled and tried to get out from under him. But he was no longer the same person, but someone else all the way. He squeezed the woman's throat with one hand and hit her face with the other. Oh, how he missed the feel of real power in his arms! However, even if he could calculate the strike, he didn't think about it. The blood on the woman's face aroused him even more. He didn't pay attention to the blows of her fists against his wide chest. He hit her again. Surely this should have knocked her unconscious by now. These people were always so fragile.

But after screaming once, she called her lover's name, tried to get him back, and then the woman squeezed her teeth and did not repeat a sound so loved by the rapist. He hissed, picked her up, and threw her off the bed on the floor, intending to enter her as himself this time and finally get what he came here for.

The naked woman landed on the floor, on their scattered clothing, like a cat on all four. She rolled over, and before Morbus understood what appeared in her hand – a chunky black glove – the blond man received a deadly zapper ray right into his heart. The martyr hurried to leave the dead man before the pain in Morbus's chest became real.

Nevertheless, it was just excruciating enough to wake Matilda up and get away on the small boat before this last irreplaceable decognitivator was lost to a Great Martyr.

***

Matilda came round when the yacht was left far behind. The decognitivator was no longer in the boat. Her dinghy was flying like a good speedboat across the rather calm sea. There were almost no clouds overhead, and Matilda felt hot. She propped herself up on her elbow and shielded her eyes from Vitr's bright light. The dry wind hit her face like a whip. The red dwarf seemed much higher above the horizon, and the air was thin but heavy with steam. Her head ached, and blood no longer flowed from the cut on her forehead but rather turned into a black crust. Matilda stared at the smears on her fingers in dismay and threw her arm over the side to scoop up some seawater and cool her face. She immediately shrieked and shook her hand. The ocean was almost as hot as boiling water.

Matilda sat up and looked around. She saw only the horizon. The sky astern was a little darker. She couldn't think straight from the heat but saw the boat rushing faster than usual towards Vitr, which means south. Her ZPE converter worked like mad, and the engine roared with excess energy. Matilda grabbed the steering handle and tried to turn the boat with her last ounce of strength. It was also hot, but she ignored the burns. She pulled the handle, but the polymer at the base, though not melted, became soft and useless. Desperate and panting, Matilda grabbed her yellow shawl and covered her head. The protective fabric brought some relief, but only for a few minutes.

She understood, gave up and lay down again on the bottom of the boat. It, too, was hot, but Matilda ceased to feel it. She had no time to close her eyes when the first gust of hot wind blinded her and burned the skin on the left side of her face and her arms to blisters. But she could not scream in pain any more and did not smell baked flesh. Matilda lost consciousness again, never to wake up. The boat raced south towards the sun of this treacherous world. There were almost no islands here; birds did not fly this far, and marine life avoided this latitude. And the biggest icebergs had long melted in the belt region. Not a single person had ever been this far from the liveable zone. The poor woman was lucky enough not to realise her true loneliness in these vast waters.

32. Karlina

The weeping woman sat in front of Nat's narrow room-control board, but Nat noticed no pity, gloating or sympathy on Vist's calm face as they watched. Nor was Vist's expression indifferent. Nat decided that there was just deep understanding and nothing more.

"When she released me, I didn't see Matilda, or even the sea any more; only the road to the port and this disgusting blue thing in my hands. I wanted to break it, but I was afraid. Morbus will have more of it anyway. So I left it with Gafan by the border. I'll tell you everything! Just save my daughter! Please! That svoloch steered the boat towards Vitr with my own hands!"

Nat sighed. "I'm afraid we can't help you. According to the satellite, your daughter has already gone too far, and none of our vehicles can reach her before she crosses the equator. And even a loader can't survive there in such temperatures. If she doesn't turn the boat around by herself—"

"But you have a spaceship!" Karlina said, almost screeching.

"Not any more. And unfortunately, that's Morbus's doing too." The metallic undertones made Vist's voice sound like vengeance itself. "Why did you help the martyr? What could she offer you?"

The grief-stricken farmer clenched her eyelids so tightly that her violet face became the colour of beetroot. It looked to Nat as if she was about to faint.

"It's all my husband's fault. When we met, I had a sugar farm, and he had a toffee factory. A few years ago, he began adding dream-pear extract to sweets to increase demand for his product ..."

Mik, standing like a rock in the corner, said miserably, "We know about that. Dream pears were illegal for years for their hallucinogens! Because of Gafan Crossich, there were several cases of young children losing their self-control and stopping pursuing their purpose. Some even ran away from home. But Gafan was discovered and expelled from the civil colony."

Karlina opened her eyes and flashed Mik a piercing glare. "Yes. But those kids weren't the only ones hooked on the drug. I had to buy pears from all the villages and all the wagoners I could reach to feed Matilda's addiction. She returned from the city to the farm when she was dumped by one of your friends! What used to be her comfort food then became a nightmare!"

Mik bellowed back, "My friend you are talking about is in the hospital as we speak, and the woman he loves has to fit the new cloned heart into his chest. I believe I don't have to tell you what happened to him. Are you really going to blame everyone else but yourself? You could have asked for help with her addiction right away."

Vist looked at Mik, and he breathed more evenly.

Nat addressed the woman again. "Mrs Crossich, we already know what happened. We tracked back all the satellite footage to the cycle of the arson and even earlier. We noticed that on that cycle you and your daughter spent more time by the factory than regular pedestrians. We also know you left some coordinates there for the architexter and later the instructions on the temple employer's house wall. Tell me, were you or your daughter under the influence of Morbus's device at those times?"

Karlina howled again with her eyes closed and her face lifted toward the detention room ceiling. "It doesn't matter. She is gone ... gone ... all I had!"

Vist stepped closer and gently touched the woman's head with their fingers, and Nat saw Vist's face reflect the unbearable pain that Karlina suffered. Some wrinkles rippled on Vist's face, and their olive eyes darkened. But something happened to Karlina too. She stopped sobbing and stared at Vist with astonishment.

"What did you do to me?" she asked after taking a deep breath.

"Our physical and emotional pain have one thing in common: our nervous system. We have long learned to control physical pain, but painful emotions are much more difficult to reduce without consequence," said Vist calmly. "I've been working on this technique for a long time. Tell me, Karlina, would you be interested in some mitigation when your sentence is decided on? Considering how much you have already lost, I am sure the Grand would not mind, if you cooperate."

Karlina paused for a moment and asked, "How long will this ... technique of yours last?"

"For a few hours. I cannot and should not make it permanent. You will grieve your daughter's death," Vist replied and stood back to let Nat do his job.

Karlina nodded and turned to him. Obviously, the woman felt much better; this relief had become the most desired currency in this trade. "I am telling you now that I don't know Morbus's real reasons. At first, she sent the gadget to me just for communication. Morbus told us how to start the fire and what to write on the walls. We didn't know what those symbols meant. I swear, we also didn't know that someone was inside and died. She couldn't get to me, but Matilda easily heard Morbus's voice in her head. Mostly there were orders for complex equipment rewarded with more dream juice. Gafan was already bringing pears to us in exchange for various goods. I stripped the factory and my house of all electronics and bought some in the city to trade. One cycle, he brought me the first device, and I started to receive instructions from Morbus through Matilda's mouth. My poor girl couldn't help but do what Morbus told her. And sometimes, Morbus took her over completely, as if possessing her. I saw the device turn the village girl into a dummy, and Morbus learned that it worked better if the person was in shock or something. That's how she eventually got to me too."

Nat waited a minute then asked, "Did Morbus say anything about why Matilda has to burn the factory?"

"She wanted to hurt someone else to make them upset and cooperate. I don't know who she was talking about, but I suspect it was someone who could spy for her in the places we could not get to."

"And what do you know about the holo-card?"

"I was told to make those devices look like various items, suitable to be presented to people or delivered to the temple. Ornaments, relics, cards. But we weren't VIP enough to get to the top floors. So Morbus told us to frighten the mechanic. Matilda knew his girl, so that was easy."

"What about the herds of svolochs by the Croc's Teeth islands?"

The woman pressed her hand to her forehead. "Morbus has a different, special control over them. Perhaps over all of them at the same time. She makes them act like a swarm or a flock. They were to compromise the southern borders to distract the main city order forces. She said that the architexter himself would attend the site and leave his house unattended. I'm glad it didn't work out, though."

"What does she want from my house?" Vist asked.

"I have no idea. But she has remote access to the decognitivator from outside the city, although the device must be near the victim. Don't ask me how it works, but someone in your house was forced by her once. I don't know who."

"Do you know who made those devices?"

"Only the person's name. Davon. I can't tell you anything else."

"And the girl Melza?"

"I know nothing about her."

"Okay, thank you for your honesty."

Nat was about to conclude the questioning, but Mik suddenly said, "And what was this attack on the yacht about? What did Morbus want from Steven?"

Karlina rubbed her temples with both hands. "It didn't concern me. Matilda and Morbus started something, and they didn't tell me what. All I know is that with the latest decognitivator, Morbus was especially fascinated by the victim's senses. She even began to smell with Matilda's nose. Not just hear, but taste and even touch became available to her."

33. Morbus

Mik walked into the village dressed in simple clothing, with a small travelling bag full of personal items. The villagers kept glancing at him, but no one dared to challenge him to share his things. Taking a huge man's possessions is not the same as robbing runaway teens.

There was a risk that some former colony citizens would recognise Mik as one of the famous loaders and masters of the ordermen. But Andrea knowingly spent several hours ensuring this didn't happen. Mik looked like a typical terrenian now. His brown skin was now deep aubergine, smooth and shiny. The upper half of his face was hidden under large mother-of-pearl scales, and his head was covered with long and straight bronze strands.

A small man with a wrinkled face and strange clothes made of woven ropes, rags and leather ribbons interrogated Mik with a few standard questions. He welcomed Mik to their modest community and explained that the Great Martyr would return to the village in just two cycles. In the meantime, a healthy new villager like Mik must build his own shelter and earn food through honest work. With such a build and complexion, he was assigned to guard the village borders against possible spies and marauders. And then the Great Contagione would decide what to do with him.

Mik was tempted to play by their rules and take over someone else's house instead of building his own. For example, the shack of this little manager. Moreover, Mik was not going to stay here for long. But for the Great Martyr herself to be less concerned with him, it was necessary to portray himself as a humble and obedient servant of God. So Mik nodded grimly, painted his face and arms with white clay, as if to protect them from Vitr's radiation, then went to the opening at the edge of the village and set up a solid scout tent, to the envy of the other villagers.

For the next cycle, he listened and observed, contacted Vist occasionally, and discussed and even showed Vist what he saw. Melza had described the village in detail before disappearing, but there was no sign of her being in the Salty Village now. Asking the locals could blow his cover, but Mik noticed that during the food distribution, one of the servants took a small portion to the empty house of the martyr. It would barely be enough for one person, let alone two captives. Therefore, Mik concluded that it was most likely that the inventor Davon Marchel was still locked in the cellar.

Mik offered Vist the option that he would free Davon in Morbus's absence and then look for Melza, but Vist thought it best not to risk it and wait for Morbus's return. Even though he missed Vist a lot and wanted to go home as soon as possible, Mik waited.

Morbus soon arrived during the sleeping hours but was so busy that it took two more cycles before Mik was summoned to the big house. He was unsure what the Great Martyr Morbus Contagione would look like, but what he saw nearly knocked him off balance.

"Mik, it's alright. These eyes have never seen you," Vist said, but nobody else could hear the metallic voice.

He immediately recognised the face of the woman who had tried to poison him thirty years ago and died during that attempt. Nikolaya Gil's face, although it had greatly changed. So that's what became of her!

Mik slowly breathed out. Let the Great Martyr think he's just nervous.

Meanwhile, Morbus studied him and talked in a business-like manner. "A new guard? I've never had such big and healthy ones before. Take off your clothes."

The Great Martyr was drunk. Mik could smell dream pears on Morbus's breath. Without changing his expression, Mik took off his shirt.

"Take everything off," Morbus insisted.

When Mik stripped, she walked around him, carefully examining every part of his body. Then she said, "Not very young, but strong. Hope everything works. Listen, guard, I want to use your body. I want to feel pleasure again ... but you won't understand yet. It will be easier for you if you don't resist. Come with me. You can leave all this here."

Mik felt uneasy and almost looked back at the door. He was not afraid of the servants. He could handle the whole village if need be, even with his bare hands, but if he made a mistake now, those he came to protect could be compromised.

He followed Morbus obediently into the bedroom. He glanced around quickly and found the entrance to the secret room described by Melza.

Near the bed, Morbus stopped and suddenly sat down in a comfortable chair by the wall. "First, guard, tell me, do you like what you see?"

Watery eyes with no eyebrows pointed at the bed. And then Mik saw that the bed was not empty. On it lay a naked girl's body on her stomach. It was Melza. Her face and long hair were smeared with white clay again. She was breathing evenly, her eyes closed. Mik leaned over and carefully examined her face. It immediately became clear to him that this was not a natural sleep. He looked closer and saw two yellow-orange spots on her shoulder blade. There may have been more such goon-fly bites, but they were not visible to him.

"She's just a child," said Mik.

"Good. So she will make noise and struggle. I'm not at all interested in her unconscious. It is much harder to find a suitable man with what I need, who would allow me to share all the sensations until I'm satisfied. If he's weak in the head, he doesn't know how to enjoy himself properly. And if he is smart, he does not let me in, and then I have to frighten and hurt him until he does. But then again, he would be unable to do the job."

"I don't understand," Mik lied.

Morbus sighed. "Nobody understands. Look at me!"

She stood up and opened her long tunic. By the number of wrinkles and pale spots, one might think she was not just sixty years old but instead closer to two hundred. There was almost nothing left of Nikolaya's once young and athletic body; she was more of an earthling than a native colonial. Without proper protection from Vitr, her skin had lost its elasticity over years of exposure to the wildlands and clay. In some places, it was covered with old scars like claw marks, cracks, red rashes and fresh scratches. The purple pigment phioletine was produced poorly without the regular transplantation of micro-glands. The maintenance she would have received in the colony would have preserved this woman much better over the last few decades.

The drunk Morbus swayed. "This is not my body. It was forced on me, and then suffered a lot before I gained my current status. You have no idea how hard it was. It was also hard to enjoy my flesh naturally until I learned how to use it. I tried men and women, drugged and awake, whole and in pieces, but nothing was good enough. Every year it becomes more and more difficult for me to use men who are no longer aroused by this body. The last time was three weeks ago, and the time before last was three years ago. But it is not meant to be anyway. I want to taste blood with my own tongue. I want to enter that" – Morbus pointed at Melza, her voice rising with every word – "with my own dick. I want my real body back, and I will get it. I don't care what it will cost me or this cruel world. I know the loader is keeping it safe somewhere because he always keeps his word. He promised me he would store my precious possessions safely. You still don't understand, do you? Maybe it is not a bad thing. One cycle I will be me again. Until then, I need you. You will fuck her for me, and I will be right here" – Morbus pointed to Mik's forehead – "feeling what you feel."

The Great Martyr covered herself again and sat down, scratching her upper arm absentmindedly.

Mik didn't say anything. The martyr didn't need to know that he knew very well what this deprived creature was talking about. There was no doubt in his mind that he was standing in front of the most vicious, selfless and irrational being he had ever known. A human and svoloch hybrid, Pilialy or Ramus Napovni, uploaded into the body of the deceased cadet Nikolaya Gil long ago. Vist's plan for

Napovni had obviously failed. All hope was that Ramus would find a new life for himself, a second chance to appreciate what he was given. Without his incredible abilities, he could have understood his victims' feelings, developed compassion and even found a purpose in redemption.

Mik remembered that Vist was watching and listening to all this, and so he stepped closer to Morbus – or Ramus – to let the architexter see him well. I wonder what you feel now, my love, he thought. Can you see now that placing the bad guy in a harsh place full of bad guys doesn't make him good. But then, what would?

Ramus Napovni looked Mik in the eye and said, "You don't say much. I like it. Maybe you are just daft enough or smart enough to appreciate this cooperation. For a start, let's see if you can get hard."

But in that very moment, a small sound came from the secret room. A beep. A beep of an electronic device that does not belong to people banished from civilisation.

"Oh," Ramus said, getting up, his frustration and melancholic gaze disappearing. "It looks like someone has entered range. Finally! We might have to postpone your test for the time being. I have an important appointment to attend. It might be my lucky cycle! Leave now, guard. I will call for you tomorrow."

When Ramus, accustomed to having his orders obeyed without question, disappeared behind the curtain in front of the secret door, Mik told Vist that Nat could bring his people into the village. Then he put his clothing back on, wrapped Melza in a sheet, and carried her out of the house. A few minutes later, when Nat's squad controlled the village, he returned with two ordermen and entered the secret room. Between the baskets on the floor, Ramus sat with his legs crossed, as if meditating. On his head, like a crown, he wore a ring of complex devices in which lumps of blue salt were randomly inserted instead of precious stones. It was clear that Ramus was literally out of his mind. He was far away; his nostrils fluttered excitedly, and his pupils moved beneath his lowered eyelids.

"Vist, do you see this?" asked Mik quietly.

"Yes. It's amazing, but neither your implants nor the satellite can sense it. Did you find Marchel?"

"No, he should be here, under the floor."

Mik, carefully trying not to wake Ramus, lifted the rug and exposed the clay slabs. He took them out, looked under the floor with his enhanced eyes, and shook his head.

"How long ago did he die?" Vist asked him.

"Judging by how much blood he let out, and his state, just before I moved here. Zina is on her way; she will tell you more. He couldn't get out. It's too deep for a small man."

"Wait, Mik." Vist's voice had a note of sudden alarm.

"What?"

"Come closer to the wall. Yes, the cell wall."

Mik jumped down and noticed something that Vist had already spotted through Mik's especially sensitive eyes. The almost cylindrical wall of the cellar, resembling a well, was covered with lines of letters scratched into the smoothed clay. He immediately recognised earthly writing, but the language was unfamiliar to him.

"Vist, you told me that you and your colleagues write down all offerings about loading technology in cipher, using one of the languages and writing. Is this it?"

"Yes, Mik, but wait, let me read. Looks like it started there."

Vist was a fast reader. For no more than five minutes, Mik, under the architexter's direction, moved his gaze along the lines until Vist had read to the end and went silent.

Mik waited and asked. "So? What does it say? Are they Davon's scribbles?"

After a very long pause, Vist answered in a very tired voice, "Yes. My darling, you have one very important thing to do right now. You must find and destroy every vablish leaf you can find in Ramus's house. All of them. Even the clean ones. And you must also destroy these wall inscriptions. Tell me you will do this. It's important. Every single letter."

34. Death of the Loader

The assassin moved confidently and fearlessly. Unlike his unsuccessful predecessors, he didn't have to hide in the dark undergrowth of the wild lands. He didn't have to pretend to be someone else, keep up a masquerade, or be afraid of identification. After all, he wasn't there at all, physically. And the hand that will strike wasn't his. It belonged to the person who would bear the responsibility and whose fate was irrelevant.

Not only that. The killer's hand isn't holding a primitive weapon, more likely to guarantee a miss than a hit. He had a real zapper, with just one single charge, one chance, but its flawless aim was reliable and deadly. It was already been proven by experience, and the feeling that comed afterwards ...

oh, how sweet was the anticipation! To see again how the face from which life has gone was changing and was becoming a mask.

There was no one in the temple corridors at this time. Usually, someone was always working or visiting the floors of the archives and museum at all hours. But no visitor ever entered this part of the temple. On the spire's highest and relatively narrow floor, there was only the architexter's office and several study rooms. And this was where he should have been right now. And there he was.

The killer approached the glass wall that lit the room with Vitr's golden rays. Hundreds of floors lay beneath his feet; from this height, the red dwarf looked higher above the horizon, brighter and whiter. The clouds here weren't above it but below. They were like a fluffy carpet, stretching in all directions. The city dome didn't protect this part of the spire – the projector was built way below this point. There wasn't enough oxygen outside these huge windows. Here you could see the orange Vitr in the south, the remote dance of the northern lights in the opposite direction, and rare stars in the clear amethyst sky above. Here you would feel exposed to space itself, as these walls of modified glass and polymers still looked fragile and thin.

A figure in a hooded robe sat in the chair before a single holo-screen and looked into it, pursing his lips. Vist's green eyes reflected the numbers running across the screen or some dead Earth language symbols.

Noticing the killer, Vist broke away from the screen and looked up at the newcomer. "Elya? Mr Goryn? What are you doing here?"

"Mr Goryn came to settle some old scores."

With these words, the killer shot Vist directly in the heart beneath Vist's silver robe. No ucha-silk, no breastplate made of stone crab could protect against such a deadly beam. Vist fell off the chair, face down on the floor. A few bright sparks jumped off the robe folds, and a pool of red blood spread under it.

Finally! The loader was dead. Vist was no more, but the holo-screen continued to shine above the small table. Its light changed from white to soft yellow, and symbols swirled to form a holographic face. This face resembled Vist's, but was fuzzy, and it seemed to look straight into the assassin's eyes.

The assassin approached and leaned over the table, planting both hands on its smooth surface. He addressed the face. "And who are you?"

"My name is Cesario. I am an assistant to Master Vist."

"Well, now you can assist me, or the purple kid you see in front of you will be the next to die."

"So I am not talking to Elya?"

"No. He is my hands, legs and my eyes. For now."

"So I am talking to Morbus? Morbus Contagione."

"Your master knew me as Ramus Napovni. With this name, I also used to have a body. I would like both of them back. I know Vist does not keep it at home any more. My spy didn't find it in the house. So, where is it?"

"It's here."

"In the temple? I knew it!" Elya – or Ramus, to be precise – pushed off the table and stood straight.

Cesario's face raised both eyebrows and looked aside, "I mean, it's here in this room." The eyes pointed to the body on the floor, "Master Vist allowed me to use it to experience humanoid mobility, but you just took it away from me. It did hurt a lot, actually, for almost 2.8 seconds. With the weapon you used, I don't believe it will now be of any use to me ... or you, even if you take it."

Ramus stared at the screen with shock for a moment and then rushed to the body. He turned it over and saw black velvet where the face was projected earlier. It looked like Vist tricked him a second time. Long ago, he pretended to be someone else; this time, the cursed loader used a decoy. And this body. *His* body!

Ramus pulled off the velvet and wailed in horror, but his mind refused to accept the truth. He ripped off the hood and saw wrinkled, pale skin on a balding head with the remnants of long yellow hair, stiff as a wire. The unused eyelids were tightly glued, the sunken cheeks were clean-shaven, and the teeth ... were replaced by dentures. It was hard to recognise Ramus's once almost handsome face, but it was his face.

He sat on the floor, holding his corpse's upper half in his arms, and he struggled to identify his feelings. Was it horror? Grief? Fury or a new desire for revenge? Ramus wasn't sure, but he didn't feel what he should. Something new was standing in the way of this emotion. Something like a drug ... stronger than dream-pear juice or goon venom.

"Wake up, princess," Cesario's screen called out, but the voice was different.

"Wake up," said a man's voice right in his ear.

With a familiar flash, the vision moved from the device in Elya's head back to Morbus. She regained her senses but had no time to recover properly.

"It's safe to remove the helmet now," said a female voice with a French accent. "The sedative should kick in now, but we have a long way to the city, so Mik, Nat, let's hurry up."

"Do you want us to take Morbus to the hospital?" Mik asked.

"No need. Scarlett and I can examine her in your detention quarters. Take her to Kinghall."

35. Ramus Napovni

Epigraphica, offering to the temple of O'Teka RN-511

As you already know, not all changes in the DNA sequence of an organism are harmful or even detectable. I was always fascinated with those human mutations that show only in their adult behaviours, and far too late for us to do anything about it.
Ramus Napovni. Bebia's journal (erased offering) – year A.C. 1008

I loved nights. At night, my mind was sharper and faster. There is no night in this damned world. It's just a name for the geographical description of the cold half of the planet, forever turned away from the sun. I remember it was dark there. My eyes saw better, although there wasn't much to see.

Here, the day never ends. And the light here is constant. It is unchanging; it never ceases to illuminate everything. It enhances colours, emphasises shapes, and leaves no room for doubt. But it also creates shadows. These shadows are thick, and I usually manage to hide in them from annoying and stubborn purple creatures who still want to call themselves humans.

But I can't hide for long from one of them in particular. As soon as I attempt to regain my freedom and do what I want, he finds me and takes away the last thing I have left every time. I am restrained once again; this time immobilised with the help of technology. And this is justice?

Oh, how I hate him! I hate him! For just a few seconds, I was allowed to feel the triumph of victory, yet everything turned out to be another insidious masquerade. My body is destroyed, I am separated from my belongings and subjects, and I can't go home. He won't stop until he breaks me, but he will not succeed in suppressing my hatred for him.

I know he is standing close to my chair. I can hear him breathing. He is waiting. Waiting a long time. He's been testing my patience for several hours now. Why doesn't he get bored?

I am hungry, my back hurts terribly, and it is difficult to breathe with my chest constrained by the immobiliser.

Finally, I decide to open my eyes. We are alone in the room. This creature stands motionless with its eyes closed, and only the movements of its eyelids and lashes betrays activity. Well, of course. With so much data in his head, he always has something to do. I study him for a minute. Long time no see. Years haven't touched him at all. His long hair has no white strands, and his wrinkles have hardly deepened. But he looked different when we met last time. He used to be more ... positive?

The door opens, and a short person comes in and breaks the silence. I don't immediately recognise her as a bearded woman, a nordian widow I used as my spy once. Vist opens his eyes and leans towards her. She whispers something, but my hearing is not as good as it used to be. I can't make out a word. The woman looks at me with an expression I haven't seen in years. I used to see fear, respect and servility on the faces of those around me. This midget looks at me with rage and hatred that can only be compared to mine. And with contempt and ... some pity? It can't be. Her look makes me feel nauseous. I understand resentment and hatred, but pity? I don't know how to respond to such feelings.

Vist nods his thanks, and she walks out, piercing me with a last look that could burn through me like a zapper. The nauseous feeling recedes with her departure. That's better.

Vist turns to me. His face shows nothing. It is cold and calm. I close my eyes and imagine him with his skin torn off.

I hear a voice with a metallic undertone. "Morbus Contagione, Ramus Napovni or Piliali Dvali? What shall I call you now?"

"Great Martyr."

"You never did anything great. I gave you the opportunity to start over once."

I open my eyes. "You didn't give. You took from me. You promised—"

"I promised you would walk again and that you would keep your mind. I also promised to secure your possessions. I kept my word, Ramus. I took your knowledge to seal the deal. What you are facing now is the result of your choices afterwards. That exile was unavoidable."

"You threw me into a harsh, dangerous world, helpless and defenceless."

"Aren't we all born into a world like this?"

"You have had parents whose duty is to protect their children."

"You devoured all those who tried to look after you. But I hoped that by sharing the pain of your victims, you would learn sympathy and understand something."

"Ha-ha-ha." I hear my own laughter, creaky and bitter. "So I was supposed to become a hero after the beatings, the loss and envy, and the separation from everything I wanted and gained. Right?"

"No. You were supposed to learn that one's agony should not be your pleasure, that your gain should not be someone's loss, and that you only become more insatiable every time you feed on what you didn't earn."

I swear I can hear a tiny speck of emotion in Vist's voice this time. He has changed, after all.

"I don't know what bullshit you're talking about. You are a fool despite your omniscience. Anyway, it pleases me if my choices have proven your big plans for me were wrong. The almighty Vist was wrong! Wrong! Ha-ha!" I am trying hard to rejoice at this discovery, but it is not satisfying.

"Yes, I was wrong about you. I thought it was the genes of your svoloch father that contributed to your twisted nature." Vist steps closer. "You wanted to turn svolochs into your soldiers. Do you know how many died under the ice just hijacking our avions? Thousands died during station takeover attempts, and for what? They never knew. I have one in my house right now. I picked her up after you taught her and forced her to sabotage our transport. Over the last few cycles, I have learned that this species may not be what we thought they are. Your observations on the inhabitants of the crater were valuable but limited. Your understanding of the man who created them was also incomplete. He didn't just make primitive cannibals. He turned them into a self-sufficient renewable material with future potential. For hundreds of years, they lived the same life. If we leave them alone in their unchanging habitat, they will continue for centuries because they lack self-learning. In this, they are similar to my neuroware."

Vist absently raises his hand to his head and brushes a strand of hair from his face with a strangely feminine gesture. "Only that part of me that is able to come up with something new, which is I, myself – the original self – allows me to be more advanced than Cesario, whom you were lucky enough to meet. But if their conditions of existence change, their childish consciousness will also begin to mature. Astuta has already used dozens of new words and learned how to use the bathroom. Imagine what would happen if I gave them enough incentives and encouraged them to develop and exit the crater? I do not rule out that in just a couple of generations, they will differ from the colonists only physically if we offer them the opportunity. But you? I believe that the conditions in which you grew up and the fact that you were different from others served as the basis for your becoming a cruel consumer. Do you remember your Bebia? Selest was the kindest woman, but she made one serious mistake. Ever since you were born, she has been afraid of you. She loved you and feared you. They were all afraid of you at KOSI."

The mention of Bebia's name causes an old and long-forgotten ache in my mind. Vist looks at me and is probably waiting for an answer.

"So that's how it turned out!" I exclaim with sarcasm. "Everything is forgiven, and you and I will be friends forever. Am I right?"

"You are wrong. Unlike the svoloch, who has no choice and would be completely changed by external conditions, you had a well-developed nervous system and intellectual potentials inherited from your mother. You were old and smart enough to decide to become good or not. Therefore, there is no forgiveness for your actions."

"And what will you take away from me this time as punishment? Mmm? I have nothing else of worth."

For the first time in my life, I see the loader frowning, and compassion appears in his eyes. But not towards me, surely.

"Ramus, I'm afraid you have something I think you should value, and I can't let you keep it. The consequences could be unimaginable. The health worker who was just here confirmed the test result. You have a new life growing in Morbus's womb. Only I know how it happened. I read and destroyed the diary of Davon Marchel in your cellar."

My first feeling is that he's talking about someone else, not me. Vist is silent, and an almost imperceptible expression appears on his face. It's that kind of pity that I can't stand. I don't believe him. I look into those cursed green eyes and feel sick again. My head starts to hurt, and a strangely familiar feeling flows into my gut. For some reason, I remembered Karlina's heart-rending cry – the last thing I heard from her when I sent her daughter south. Terrible pain squeezes my chest. It's not physical pain. It resembles the missing Bebia, but a thousand times worse. I don't want that. I can't take it. Please! Stop it! I will do anything!

36. Exile

Outside the borders of the civil colony, Gafan slowly led the crying Karlina towards the Salty Village, supporting her by the arm. He carried a sack on his back containing the things she was allowed to take into exile from the city. The amulet was no longer among them. She practically hung on Gafan and didn't watch where she was going.

He wouldn't stop talking in a soft voice, trying to calm his ex-wife, although she didn't answer him but only sobbed and moaned. Karlina's face was already smeared with white clay, but streams of tears left dark streaks on her cheeks.

"Don't worry, it will only be hard at first, but then you'll get used to it. It's not so bad here. I understand that the longing for Tilda will never go away now. This loss has broken my whole soul too. But if the Lord wishes it, he will give us a new child to console us. Wait, wait, and don't dismiss this idea. Ponder it carefully. I want you back. Not only because I am still attached to you, despite the years of separation and how you treated me, spoke down to me, despised me. You will simply be better off with me. Here you have to go through the ritual of joining the community. This means that your things now belong to all the villagers. And your body belongs to any man who wants to share a roof with you and a cycle's ration. I can protect you if you stay with me."

Karlina groaned and lowed herself on the road, but Gafan forced her to get up and walk again.

He continued, "Now that Morbus Contagione is gone, who is the real exile and proper sufferer in the village? I am! Yes, my dear! Gafan Crossich is the leader of the community. I am a Great Martyr now and I conduct a good begging service regularly. The villagers are happy with me. I do not frighten them and share food much more fairly than Contagione used to. I put things in order in the village; I don't force anyone to work so hard, and I don't torture them. I lifted them up from their knees and drove out the demons that Morbus forced into them. You called me a fool and a loser, but here I am, smarter than the others. Even that possessor device didn't pierce my mind. I am loved and respected. Believe it or not, I now live in Morbus's house. All the furniture and other things you and I smuggled to the village will now be ours. We are now a family again. You are my wife. Nobody dares to even look at you. Listen to your husband, do what you are told, and everything will be fine."

37. Timofey

Timofey Hesley noticed that recently Vist switched off their amulet more often and for longer. As they didn't answer the conv-call, he was looking for the architexter in a rather unusual way. He knew Vist was now with one of his friends but did not know with whom. Therefore, the temple satellite overseer briefly connected to each amulet to find the answer to the question, but he did so in such a way that would not distract anyone or overhear a personal conversation. Only he had this urgent access to the colonists' amulets, and he used it only in cases of urgent need. It was impossible not to hear snatches of phrases, but Mr Hesley had a truly pressing matter to solve.

First, he came across the voice of Elya Goryn, who was talking to the daughter of Rod Baker somewhere near Paradise Garden. His voice was full of pride and daring. Apparently, his audience was listening wide-mouthed. "And if the colonists practically corrected Captain Darkwood's eyesight on their first visit, your father's new finger, bitten off by the svoloch, was cloned and fixed only upon his return. We stopped making mech-limbs by then and completely replaced them with organic implants. So one cycle I started thinking—"

Then Timofey heard a phrase that Rod Baker himself said to the woman with whom he had dinner on Thursdays. "Of course, that made me change my mind. I cannot let Obydva raise the child alone. I am not that useless, after all. My dear Lariona, your ancestor and I did things on Earth during the resistance that would shock you. Wesley loved to repair machinery that everyone else considered hopeless. Even I—"

Timofey felt a little uncomfortable when he heard his sister and her husband talking in their house. Nat said, "Something happened between them after we left. I could sense it on the very next cycle! Can you imagine?"

And Andrea replied, "No. But does that means Vist is a woman?"

"It does not!"

Timofey turned his head a few degrees to the left and heard Dr Zina's voice. "Stop apologising. I know it wasn't you in that moment. I knew it from the first second. You better hug me, Steven, right now. A broken heart hurts, but try to grow a new one! It hurts even more. I know that. We will succeed—"

Timofey found Obydva soon after that, saying, "Mik, you won't believe it, just as I didn't believe my eyes. Those clones were sitting at the table, holding hands. I would have thought it was Chang himself if it weren't for the skin colour. He looked almost like an exact copy of Broadsky, tinted with ink. He smiled at the woman. But I only worked out her face under the hairy forehead when I brought them dessert. If you shaved her, she would have been Marta's spitting image. Mik, they met here. They found each other, and they are together. Despite all time and space. And you can call me a sentimental blobster, but I decided at that very moment!"

Finally, Timofey heard what he was searching for. "Master Architexter, but I only have a year left before the elections. I would like to do as much as possible for the colony's security. Those villagers have again revived old plans and attempts that are becoming increasingly sophisticated."

Timofey lingered there longer and heard an answer with a metallic undertone. "It's not the villagers themselves that threaten us. They simply chose such a simple way of life as an outcome of their aimlessness. Their leaders, they stir them up in their passivity and envy. But, as expected, the time has come when the townspeople can no longer be relied upon as much. I promise that all satellites will be programmed to monitor trade between villages and signs of smuggling from now on."

Timofey stopped listening, passed the message to the Grand's amulet that he would be there soon, and headed towards the mayor's residence. He went on foot because his journey from the temple took under five minutes, although he wanted to get there in five seconds. Vist was waiting for him in their conmot. She or he was now alone.

"Judging by you being out of breath, you have something urgent to tell me?" Vist asked with a smile instead of a greeting.

Timofey sat on the passenger seat, saying, "Yes, see for yourself, master."

He held out his hand. Vist squeezed Timofey's wrist amulet lightly and closed her eyes. Timofey watched as one of the broad eyebrows rose first, then the other, and then Vist frowned and let go of his hand.

"You found him!" said the metallic voice, trembling slightly, "Tom is alive."

"At least he was two hours ago. Master, it's very far away. What shall we do?"

"We're going to need new transport. Our *Wasp* is stuck under the ice, and the Bumblebag, which could lift her, is resting on the ocean floor. The colony's other vehicles are not designed for our needs."

"I'm sure Cesario won't have trouble—"

Vist looked his apprentice straight in the eye, and he fell silent.

"Tim, when I tested your great-great-grandfather, I didn't expect him to pass the test. Only another loader of my build or an independent neural mesh could handle it. I was very surprised when a young colonist solved it a few generations later without a single artificial cell in his head. You've dug into the archives of everything a human might know with incredible diligence and have exceeded my expectations. I can't say exactly what helped you: easier access to knowledge, a special gene, maybe your way of using an amulet, your human passion, stubbornness and obsession? I don't know, but you proved your worth then and have done it again. It is time for you to take the position of architexter. Are you ready for such an upgrade?"

Timofey beamed, and he couldn't immediately answer. "I didn't even hope! Of course."

"Cesario works fast but can't come up with anything new despite having access to all of humanity's blueprints. The conditions we need to get into to bring Captain Darkwood home are a whole gamut of new factors that O'Teka knows nothing about. You have an advantage."

"But I'm not an engineer and can't invent anything."

"If you can be loaded with everything I have, you can invent. I can, Rod Baker can, and with such a network of knowledge and talents, we can do it in a cycle and bring Steven a new scheme before he leaves the hospital. I have enough funds to buy materials and the best plant to build it. Prepare yourself. Tomorrow I will insert into your system everything you need and wire you up. Be warned, it will be quite a shock, but you will recover quickly. Unlike me, you won't have to replace body parts because of tissue rejection. We will find Tom. He managed to survive there for five years, eleven months and twenty-one cycles. He seems to be doing well and can wait for another few weeks."

The protective screen over the city slowly darkened, depicting an artificial cloudless evening with constellations from Earth's northern hemisphere. In its dome above the temple, a huge timer was shining, displaying 18.12. On the square, a dozen white doves, sparrows and tetrapteryxs began to settle down to rest on the backs of the benches among the small trees.

Vist started the conmot, crossed the square, and dropped their apprentice off by the temple, still talking excitedly about what would be done in the next week or so. Timofey got out of the vehicle and, despite being overwhelmed with feelings, noticed that Vist turned not towards their house but towards somewhere else entirely.

"Master, where are you going now, if not to the temple?" he asked.

"Today, you know what to do without me, and I have plans. General King invited me to dinner. We'll talk tomorrow."

To be continued

Book 4: *Who Was Vist* – **Official Trailer**

The svoloch could not survive such a blast. Maybe another loader could and – of course – it didn't work.

He raised his head and listened. These were human steps approaching him, confidently but slowly. Nothing could be seen in the mixture of smoke and fog. Nat rose to his full height, cursing the pain in his back, and prepared to fire. In the white cloud, a shapeless silhouette first appeared, which took on the outline of a man of short stature and wide clothing with a hood thrown back. The approaching person looked beneath their feet and tried not to step on the corpses.

At the sight of the figure in a robe with a thick locks of chestnut hair, Nat cried with joy, wanting to grab the loader in his arms. But he restrained himself and only asked with a tremor in his voice, "Vist?"

The olive eyes turned to him, and Nat realised he was mistaken. The resemblance was startling, but this face was younger, darker, with fuller lips and no shaved temple.

"No," a velvety female voice answered him. "I am the daughter of the person you are looking for."

"Daughter?" Nat mumbled in shock.

"Yes. Vist was my—"

ABOUT THE AUTHOR

Anka B. Troitsky was born in the USSR in 1968, grew up in Kazakhstan and left for the UK in 1993.
She writes science fiction and fantasy novels, and short stories in various genres, including LGBTIQA+.
She is the author of the first two novels in the series (Object and Vist, Construct and Vist), already available on KDP and Audible.

Other work in English (short stories):

Belmère

Up the Wormhole

The St Petersburg's Renaissance

Author's website: www.ankatroitsky.com

Printed in Great Britain
by Amazon

35723970R00188